HOW TO BE A FOOTPIG

by James T. Medak

NOTE: Under no circumstances should you read this book unless you yourself are barefoot.

TABLE OF CONTENTS

INTRODUCTION

This book would not have been possible were it not for someone whom I will probably never actually get to meet.

Prior to me writing my first word of erotica, I was, of course, a rabid consumer of hot stories. It didn't matter if they were on forums, internet archives, or actual story sites, but in some ways the written word wound up conjuring up some of the horniest sensations I ever had, as that right amount of deviousness or that perfect turn of phrase wound up working its mojo on me better than any any porn clip ever could. Of course, erotica as a "genre" is often treated as a trashy disposable thing largely because, well, it is: it's an outlet for the desperately horny to get their thoughts down, and, unsurprisingly, a lot of it is unfocused, if not horrendously unskilled. For every good piece of erotica you ever read, there are at least a dozen examples of bad erotica, pretty much like any literary genre. This is nothing new.

Therefore, I wound up becoming extremely impressed with those who took it seriously, who devoted time and consideration to their efforts, who maybe went as far as to divvy things up into chapters so that there's an actual buildup and flow like a proper story should have. Certain works, like "The Wall" by the writer only known as Eddie or "Frat House Interrogation" by the guy known known as Ratty (there were a lot of single-name authors at the time) wound up taking on an iconography all their own, referenced in numerous posts across several years, and for good reason: they were genre high points, the best (and horniest) of them all. These people took well-worn tropes and treated them with all the tension and suspense of a Tom Clancy spy thriller, and they imprinted the minds of several young men like myself in incalculable ways.

There was always one story, though, that I kept coming back to time and time again. It was called "College Foot Slave" by a writer who was only known as Tommy and who never left any contact information at all.

The crux of the story (which, it should be noted, can still be found on

MyFriendsFeet.com's free story archive page) involves a young guy who writes lots of letters to himself about how attracted he is to guy's feet and how much he hates being tickled. One day at the campus library, he finds his laptop stolen, found by the hot and horny jock dom of the resident frat on campus, and instead of leaking all of his dirty secrets out to the public, they make him sign an extensive, devious contract that basically ensures he'll be the frat's personal sex slave for a long long time, forced to lick feet, give blowjobs, be humiliated for their amusement and so much more. The setup was the most fucking devious thing I had ever read; what irked me was the way that it played out.

Make no mistake, "College Foot Slave" is an incredible, insanely long, ridiculously hot story, but I have never developed a real taste for cruelty. I don't mind doms by any means -- fuck, I love obeying me some orders from a guy with some naked feet to be truly proud of -- but being mean for the sake of being mean without any regard for the feelings of the sub has always been something that I could never really get behind. I truly believe that in dom/sub play, both parties can easily work to their mutual satisfaction, even if harsh punishments and language is used in order to get there. In "College Foot Slave", the jocks wind up using and abusing the lead character in some very hot ways and some slightly disturbing ways -- I was never able to give it a full-on ringing endorsement for its content even if its initial idea was one that kept me cumming back to it again and again.

Previously, when I was starting out putting my stories on the TKLFrat forums and getting a surprisingly strong response to them, I was asked by certain community members to actually write "sequels" to some existing stories by other writers on MyFriendsFeet, as apparently my aesthetic resonated in such a way that some people wanted to see what I might do at handling continuations of those existing tales. I felt I did a good job serving as a modern "interpreter" for these stories, and that inherently lead me to have the confidence to do something along the lines of adapting a story as great as "College Foot Slave" -- but I never once imagined that adaptation would ever be a complete, novel-length work in and of itself.

In many ways, starting out as writing short stories seemed to be the best fit for erotica, because the stories often got to the point and by their very nature didn't have a lot of time to linger -- after all, an erotically charged reader may only have an "attention span" for a short amount of time, if you catch my drift. This is why my first two books, *How to Be a Tickle Slave* and *My, What Ticklish Feet You Have* were nothing but short story compilations -- it just made the most logistical sense.

Yet when *Getting Off on the Wrong Foot* came out in 2013, the entire back half of the book was a single narrative story ("The Market"), an amalgam of so many horny thoughts and ideas all bound together in one place. Continuing the self-imposed rule of never writing the same "type" of story twice, exploring a more ambitious narrative, with, of course, all the horny deviousness I had become known for, was very appealing. Had I not been able to do that, I wouldn't have been able to tackle what you're reading right this very moment: a much more sprawling and satisfying story that is (I hope) both epic and ambitious in scope.

While certain tropes of my own are still apparent (including my horrible yet uncontrollable habit of writing real-life friends as characters as I see fit), titling the book *How to Be a Footpig* was itself something I needed to do. Curiously, one of the strange side-effects of becoming a vaguely (and boy do I mean vaguely) prominent member of this community was the sheer number of people that reached out to me to "thank" me for being as open and outgoing as I have been about having a foot fetish. While sometimes the mind may be clouded with thoughts of overarching dom/sub play, simply being an outspoken "representative" for the fetish meant something to certain people, that it was *totally OK* to be in lust with male feet and not feel like a freak of nature. More than anything, amidst our protagonist's many adventures into the world of forced podiacal servitude, I wanted to convey a narrative that having this fetish doesn't define you: it's a part of you that just needs to be embraced. People shouldn't be afraid of their sexuality: it's just one aspect of the rich tapestry that is each person's life. In essence: I fucking love male bare feet to death -- so what?

I have spent literally months upon months working on this book, and to finally see it meet the light of day is nothing short of astonishing. I do profoundly hope you enjoy, footpigs -- 'cos I sure as goddamn hell enjoyed writing it.

Feet dreams.

--James T. Medak
July 2014

This book is dedicated to all my friends who have indulged me in pattering on about my fetish, their own feet, and basically putting up with me for as long as they have. It may seem like a small thing but it means a lot to me. You know exactly who you are, and trust me, I am beyond grateful. This is for you.

CHAPTER ONE: How to Operate a Footboner

Tom's footboner was absolutely throbbing.

He couldn't concentrate. Hell, he was embarrassed that he couldn't concentrate. Yet there he was, right there in the middle of his college library in the dead of night, sitting in an isolated table of the library's main study wing, nursing a raging, pulsing erection inside of his gray slacks. Overwhelmed with humiliation, Tom felt that couldn't hide his tent from any angle, and he was starting to panic.

The whole reason Tom went to the library in the first place was to avoid distractions. Back in his dorm room, his roommate, Theron, a somewhat-burly red-haired gamer type who happened to do a lot of behind-the-scenes work in the college's theatre department, was a little drunk, as was his norm. Theron was a smart guy, a fun guy for sure, but tonight must've been a particularly rough one for him at the theater (it was tech week, Tom was told), as not only was Theron hitting the red wine pretty hard, but he also had taken his dark socks off to drunkenly chillax while watching a movie in their tiny dorm room, feet propped up on a purple milk crate that somehow found its way into their humble abode.

Theron was one of those guys who never went barefoot, would rather cut off an appendage before ever buying a pair of sandals, and Tom was certain that there more than a few nights when he actually slept in socks. Yet for Theron, with his masculine build and sensitive soul, it was rare for him to do something as simple as prop up his pale bare feet in front of the TV, and catching the sight of those raw soles coated in the blue hum of the tube -- well, it made Tom melt. He couldn't *not* look at them. He stared intently, his eyes absolutely drinking in the sight. Every toe twitch, every rubbing of his bare foot flesh together and the slight scraping sound it produced -- it was close to overwhelming.

While Tom knew that for most of his life he out-and-out loved the mere sight of bare male feet, in that exact moment, it was consuming him, completely taking control of his every cognitive function. Tom looked at the plumpness of Theron's toepads, the soft, pale undersides of each toe midsection, the delicious shade of pink that was developing on the ball of Theron's feet -- and it utterly intoxicating. In that light, in that moment, Tom would be willing to get a tattoo of those feet somewhere on his person and he would never second-guess it.

Fuck, he had to get out of here before it got any worse.

Tom quickly stood up and tried to do so in a graceful way so as not to reveal the sudden, raging erection that was trying to break through his slacks. He closed his laptop and scooped it quickly in his messenger bag along with the charger. Theron's face, covered in orange unshaven scruff, lazily tilted over in Tom's direction.

"Where you going buddy?" inquired Theron, taking a sip of wine straight from the bottle as he did so.

"Oh, I'm ... I'm a bit distracted. I think I need to go to the library to study," Tom stammered, a bit flummoxed.

"Don't lie," Theron jokingly lazed, "it's the smell of my feet, ain't it?"

Tom's dick twitched at the very sound of that sentence hitting his ear. The very thought of Theron's masculine footmusk was too much for him. Even in trying to strategically position his tan messenger bag over his pulsating meatrod, he could swear that Theron noticed that involuntary throb through the bag itself. Tom's face was going beet-red with embarrassment at record pace.

"Oh no," Tom said with an awkward smile plastered on his face. "I just ... if I don't start studying now ... I don't think I'll ever start."

"Suit yourself," Theron said, taking another swig, "Hasta mañana." At this point Theron "waved goodbye" with his right foot. Tom's eyes widened: he had to leave *right the fuck now if he wanted to keep an semblance of sanity*. He bolted.

As he ran out into the dorm hallway and closed the door behind him, he placed his back right up against the wall just outside his room. Tom was heavily panting. His arms were even trembling a bit, simply overwhelmed by what he just saw. Having a male foot fetish was something he accepted, and after doing research on the various psychological aspects of it (including, most terrifyingly, that it is something that'll you'll probably have for the rest of your life), he grew to simply embrace it instead of trying to run from it. However, here in his college dorm hallway, after seeing Theron inexplicably push all his buttons, Tom almost felt like he was out of control. If he stayed in that room 10 seconds longer, his fetish would overwhelm him, take over his body, and make him do things to his roommate that were not the most appropriate in nature, humiliating him forever. After taking in a few more steadying breaths, Tom collected himself, and made his way over to the campus library to study, adjusting his pants as he went so that his erection wasn't too visible.

+ + +

At first, the dual task of studying and forgetting about Theron's unbelievably attractive bare feet was going surprisingly well. By immersing himself into his textbook on 1800s European History, Tom was able to get the start of a paper outline done, did an online quiz for class, and made some progress on the chapter that he needed to finish for the next class. He felt good about these accomplishments, and in order to celebrate such miniscule accomplishments, he pulled a granola bar out from his messenger bag, started chewing on it, and decided to just check his Facebook page as part of his break.

He began scrolling through pictures and posts of crazy viral videos that people were sharing, the occasional over-emotional status update, that one post from your politically-minded friend which debunked whatever popular narrative was currently taking over this current news cycle -- all the usual. He then saw that Matt, one of the hottest guys on campus, was tagged in a few new photos. Matt had a nice build to him: short, dusty brown hair, a solid body that looks like it was carved from years of featherweight wrestling (note: Matt never wrestled, he just looked like that), and -- oh gods, he was wearing shorts and flip-flops in this recent batch of photos. Greedily, Tom began pawing through the new images, particularly enjoying how Matt's lightly-tanned skin looked nice against the crude blue of his cheap budget-bin sandals. Each click through displayed those sexy digits of his at different angles, sometimes painfully out of frame, and then there was one -- in one of those mis-clicked camera pics that somehow made its way into the upload folder -- that was almost pointing right down at Matt's bare, sandaled foot, center frame, and holy hell did it look good.

Fuck that: it looked better than good. It looked sexy. Slowly, Tom could simply feel that tingly sensation in his balls start to percolate, growing slowly, engorging his member. This picture of Matt's foot was beautiful. It was perfect. It was God. Immediately without even thinking, Tom pulled open a draft document file he had been saving: his fun little private writing he had done about what it'd be like to be subservient to Matt. It was an ongoing little document he had been working on for some time, and he opened it up periodically because when it came to describing his fantasies, as he found he was much better expressing his horniness with the written word than in any other format. Although Matt was well-liked on campus, Tom had heard enough rumors that Matt was kind of aggressive, a bit of a dick to girls at times (even after he slept with them), and was a known prankster. There were even scarcer rumors that one he had a hookup with a guy on campus, which was interesting given how he is known as quite the pussy-loving lothario. Still, all of this was just painting a vivid picture in Tom's mind and he had to get these thoughts together.

As he typed furiously in this document, the scenario became vivid: Tom kneeling on the hardwood floor of Matt's frat-house, Matt sitting there in a chair, loosening the sandal from his foot and placing that sole right down on the center of Tom's face, applying a good amount of pressure, saying "That's right bitch, sniff it. You love the smell of my feet, don't you? You little foot freak. Show me what a fuckin' freak you are." As Tom typed this, an elaborate description of being humiliated with his own fetish in front of his object of desire, he could barely keep his own footboner from growing. Underneath the desk of his massive study room, he was sporting serious steel, and were he not so involved in what he was writing, he'd make more deliberate efforts to hide it from view. Yet, here he was, adding more to his Matt story in a computer folder that was filled with dozens of such missives. Some of them confessions about how much he hates being tickled, some professing how much he'd like his foot fetish used against him, others just hot scenarios of him sucking a particular guys' toes and sniffing that man's worn college sandals in an effort to get off (or, even better, sniffing those sandals while in his room alone before being "walked in on"). They were all a bit scattered, some more "focused" than others, but all true expressions of what he was feeling, and a very safe environment to explore even more contours of his sexuality.

Tom eventually stopped, his boner straining against the front his pants to the point where it almost hurt. He had to relieve himself. Doing his best to stand while adjusting his boner so it lay vertical, pointing to his belly button whilst under his pants, he walked across the study room and down the stairs of the library's basement. Down there were the restrooms, and being late night at a college library, there weren't a lot of people who come in and potentially disturb any acts of self-pleasuring. The restroom was pretty darn clean, the walls to the stalls made from marble for some reason (must've been some donors' pet project), and although a bit thinner than a standard men's stall, Tom found a really clean one, went in, and closed the heavy wood door behind him.

He immediately undid his belt and unzipped his pants, too-eager to unleash his throbbing member out in the air. There it was: already beet-red, veins prominent, eager for release. Tom took a few quick tugs at it, just to keep it in the state it was: tingly, eager, and absolutely controlling the entirety of Tom's attention. With his pants down to his knees, Tom hastily reached in his left pants pocket to pull out his smartphone, and proceeded to scroll through it, looking at all the various candid foot photos he had taken now and then: social events, parties, even standing in line at the college cafeteria. Tom ran a small candid foot blog where he would occasionally post these pictures, because truth be told, he found it extremely hot that a guy, by wearing sandals, would have absolutely no idea that photos are being snapped of his bare toes, posted online, and then jerked off to by hundreds if not thousands of foot pervs the world over. That idea -- of the completely unknowing, unwilling straight sexgod -- was very appealing to Tom, which is why he was close to maxing out the hard drive space on his phone, candid, unbeknownst toe and sole shots galore contained within.

He narrowed in on one that he quite liked, that of a handsome guy named Thomas who seemed to wear sandals everywhere at all times, despite being rail-thin and having a bit of nice scruff to his face, and boy was it delicious. He then scrolled one over to the tops of a guy in his socioeconmics class named Taran, who had meaty, meaty size 11s with prehensile toes. Tom, now jacking furiously at the pixels on his screen, had the image of Taran's toes so vividly in his head that his eyes rolled up, his lids closed, and he squirted out one cumshot after another, awash in a realm of absolute, unquestionable footpleasure. He indulged his fetish to the nth degree, but christ was it worth it.

After a few heavy pants, Tom's head started to clear, started adjusting to "reality," and he could see that his hot seed had gotten over the front of his pants. "Fuck," he uttered. Still with no presence in the bathroom outside of him and his own horniness, Tom pulled his pants back up, went over to the sink and spent an inordinate amount of time both washing the cum from his pants but also drying them with numerous paper towels so he could return to his study area without any potential embarrassment. He could've sworn he went through half of the paper towels in the dispenser to accomplish this, but the results spoke for themselves.

Tom walked back upstairs and into the main study hall where he was sitting about a half hour after the fact, and he could see where he was sitting ... but his computer was gone. The charger, strangely, still remained, as well as his messenger bag, but his computer was nowhere to be scene. Panicked, his eyes darted around the room, looking for any potential suspects, any sign that the cleaning people may have moved it while he was away ... but there was nothing. Absolutely nothing. Gradually, Tom's face started to flush with blood, worry and embarrassment setting in. He did two complete walkabouts of the entire library, looking for something, anything that would indicate where his laptop was, but tragically, it was to no avail.

Tom for a moment just slumped over in the chair he was studying at earlier, burying his face in his crossed arms, almost ready to release some sobs over the whole situation. His work that he was doing: gone. His save drafts for his projects in class: gone. Everything was gone. Tom flat-out felt miserable, and didn't move for a full 20 minutes, just letting that weighty feeling of depressing sink in, gradually accepting that there was nothing he could do about this absolutely shitty situation.

Eventually, realizing that moping wasn't going to help solve the problems at hand, he picked himself up and went back over to his dorm room. By the time he got in, Theron was snoring heavily, that bottle of wine having apparently treated him rather nicely. Tom simply threw his messenger bag down, set his alarm, and crawled into bed, defeated. Maybe he'd feel better in the morning ... but probably not.

+ + +

The next day, Tom groggily got up, having gone through some weird nightmares that he couldn't fully articulate (something about a dagger that turned into a synthesizer that soon attacked a village), and got to the communal shower before getting dressed and heading over to class. He tried to be on auto-pilot as much as possible because he very much did not want to think about the sheer amount of work he'd have to do now that his laptop was gone. He grabbed a health food bar from the local campus eatery, and soon was off to his first class of the day, World Philosophy, which itself was quite the snoozefest. Being how it was still early Fall, there were quite a few guys in the class who decided that wearing flip-flops would be a good idea, and Tom would have to degree. Being in a desk in the middle of the class made it close-to-impossible to snag a candid shot, but truth be told, Tom wasn't much in the mood for that kind of naughtiness today.

At his college, there was a good 20-minute space between classes, so Tom took time between World Philosophy and Intro to Biochemistry to swing by the mail room, see what campus flyers and other whatnot he was going to throw away today. When he got to the crowded mailroom, he got to his box on the massive wall they had for all students, entered his combo, and opened it up, only to see a small folded note inside. He pulled it out and opened it up: there was a picture of his laptop printed on it, screen open, showing ... a picture of feet?

Tom just stared at the image. Then stared at it some more. He *knew* what it was, but his brain almost refused to accept the idea. Then, it did: oh fuck.

Indeed, right there on this printed picture was a candid photo of some male feet, the one of Matt in his sandals that he swiped off of Facebook, and it was full-screened. Being this was a photo of a computer monitor, the image was a bit blurry, but he could clearly see some guy's index finger pointing to the screen, somewhat in an "OMG look at this!" kind of way. Tom's worst fear ever had been realized: he had been found out.

Tom couldn't have blushed any more than he was doing so right now. A terrible feeling washed over him: an absolute, bone-shakingly terrifying fear of being exposed, mocked, ridiculed at large. His friends' emails were saved on that computer. His *parents* emails were saved on that computer. His Facebook password was saved on that computer. *Everything* was saved on that computer, including his candid photos, his videos downloaded from porn sites, and -- oh god -- the letters. All the letters he wrote to himself. They were all there. Tom's heart-rate began pumping rapidly, that overwhelming sense of humiliation leaving him cold and alone, moreso than he had ever felt in his entire life.

He glanced at the note again and saw there was writing underneath it: "TKL Frat House. 8pm. TONIGHT."

Dear gods, someone was holding his laptop for ransom. This was ever possible flavor of "not good" ever conceived. Tom's mind was rushed with ideas, most of them utterly paranoid, but all completely justified in this situation. He would've dived even further down the hole of torment were it not for the campus-wide bell going off, informing everyone that it was time to move to the next period.

The rest of the day was completely and utterly useless for Tom: although he sat there in class scribbling notes like an automaton, absolutely none of the information presented was entering his brain. All he could feel was a hot, burning sensation in his skull that he couldn't shake out, one that radiated with worry and concern. Tom was often a very organized person, but he had absolutely no idea how tonight was going to turn out, and that's what concerned him more than anything else: the fear of the unknown.

Later, as he was going through the dinner-line in the campus cafeteria, not even caring what was being served on his tray, his brain kept floating to his encounter tonight. He kept looking at the clock on his phone, counting down the hours before the inevitable, but while Tom was legitimately scared by his pending evening of what was going to no doubt be insane humiliation as he tried to get his laptop back, there was a part of him -- a part he was desperately trying to fight and vehemently deny -- that was, to be honest, kind of turned on by what could very well happen. It was very much like one of the letters he had written, but those were things that were to be kept strictly in the realm of fantasy. This ... this was something else entirely.

Around 7:30pm, having not gone back to his room all day specifically to avoid Theron, Tom went by to drop off his messenger bag, in hopes that it too wouldn't be stolen upon his arrival at the frat house. When he got in, Theron was on his computer, and from the side glance that Tom unconsciously gave, he could see that underneath the computer chair, sticking out of the pants of blue jeans, Theron was, once again, barefoot. This was so unlike him, to be unshod two days in a row, but Tom tried to push it out of his mind while removed his messenger bag from his shoulders.

"You're in late," Theron noted, not glancing away from his computer screen. "What's going on?"

"Oh," Tom said, trying to sound as calm and "normal" as possible, "just got some stuff I gotta take care of. Heading out tonight."

"Yeah, but your Science Club doesn't meet on Wednesdays," said

Theron, surprising Tom with knowledge of his own schedule.

"Um, yeah, but I gotta meet up with some guys," Tom said, sheepishly.

"When you gonna be back?" Theron still wasn't looking away from his monitor.

"Um ... I dunno! But, um, I gotta get going, OK?" Tom now was making his way for the door.

Theron's head turned to face Tom. "Is everything OK, man?"

"Yeah, no, it's just ..." and Tom started walking away.

"Hey!" Theron shouted as he was leaving, something that Tom heard but chose to ignore. He didn't want to answer any more questions: the fact that he was walking to the frat house now, the frat house that contained his computer full of dirty secrets, was humiliation enough. The last thing he wanted to do was talk to his roommate about how bad his footcrush on him was -- something that may or may not come to light depending on how the rest of the night played out. That idea was actually the scariest of all ...

CHAPTER TWO: Terms & Conditions

For some reason, against the night sky, the TKL frat house looked a bit intimidating. The lights in front, the pale darkness of a cloudy night sky behind it -- it seemed like a postcard you'd buy from some tourist-bait haunted house. Nervous to the point of trembling, Tom walked forward, slowly, preparing for his inevitable doom. Step-by-step up towards the door, hanging his head down in shame before knocking on it twice. There was a thickness and hollowness to the door, making it really feel like he was about to enter a dungeon -- which wasn't entirely off the mark, truth be told.

The door creaked open. "Hello there," a voice said. "Now get the fuck inside."

Tom walked inside and felt the hulking door close (and lock) behind him. He was in the main room of the frat-house, a light wood-paneled floor beneath his sneakered feet, a trashy couch and large-screen TV hung up on the wall, doors leading to other places, a stairway right in the middle of the first floor.

Tom's eyes first darted and connected with the face of the person who let him in: Red. A born frat boy, Red was a star on the college's football team, and although he didn't have a "bulky" build, he still had a powerful frame, stood six feet tall, and, of course, had buzzed red hair donning his head. He was a natural ginger, and some had said that this may be the reason behind his own fiery temperament. As Time glanced at his body, however, his eyes couldn't help but dart down to his feet, and sticking out of Red's dark-blue denim jeans were his pasty bare feet snuggly fitting in a pair of stylish flip-flops. Tom darted his eyes back up to Red's as quick as he could, as he didn't want his pupils to linger on the jock's masculine toes for too long, although Red's firm smirk knew more than it let on.

"Yeah, you like what you see down there, boy?" Red said, wiggling his toes in his sandals.

"Please," Tom said meekly, "can I just have my laptop back?"

"Oh, is the bitch here?" shouted a voice from the kitchen.

"Oh yes!" Red declared, "And man, you should see how hard he's trying *not* to stare at my toes right now. It's fucking hilarious."

"Lemme see," said the voice, drawing nearer. Wiping his hands with a dish-towel, Tom now caught a glimpse of a young guy with ink-dark hair, a shorter stature, but a rather muscular frame. He was wearing thick horn-rimmed glasses, but in combination with his hair, he looked like a sexy young Clark Kent (or just a cruising Jimmy Olsen). "Oh man, look at him! He's like a scared puppy!" The man was pointing.

"I know, Dave!" said Red, both men now talking to Tom as if he wasn't in the room. "He's just so goddamn embarrassed. We're gonna have fun now, aren't we?"

"Oh yes," said Dave, tossing the dish-towel in the general direction of the kitchen, not giving a damn if it made it or not. Dave then plopped down on the sofa length-wise, his own sneakered feet hanging off of the armrest.

"Hey Matt!" Dave shouted upstairs. "The entertainment has arrived!"

There was no audible response to this, aside from the sound of footsteps rumbling down a staircase that was nearby but must've been in another hallway altogether. Suddenly, in a plain t-shirt, board shorts, and cheap blue flip-flops, there was Matt, the dusty-blonde badboy with a nice set of muscles and a wicked grin -- just as how Tom always envisioned him, acting and looking from all those Facebook photos he downloaded of him. Matt immediately locked eyes with Tom, who averted his gaze downward, still keeping Red's sandaled toes in his frame of vision, albeit barely.

"Man, it kind of makes sense, lookin' at him," Matt declared, moving towards the kitchen. "I mean, I still don't believe it, but this is gonna be fun." Matt returned with a beer bottle in hand, soon sitting down on a nearby comfy chair, his eyes pointing at the shy boy in the frat house's foyer, scared to even acknowledge that there were three handsome jock guys looking right at him. Red, Dave, and Matt. Tom's heart was pounding like a jackhammer right now, but he was doing all he could to not make it look visible. He was trying so hard not to think about why he was here, much less that these were men who all apparently knew his secret, and, worse of all, knew how badly they could use it against him.

"Sit on the floor next to Dave, boy," Red said, walking towards another comfy chair while Tom simply plopped down on the floor, back against the couch, Dave's shoe-covered feet still dangling off of the armrest but still dangerously close to his head.

Tom looked around: Dave was staring at him from the couch behind him, Matt was sandal-clad in the chair on his left, and Red was sitting in a chair on his right, those meaty toes looking snug in those thick sandals of his. It was a Bermuda Triangle of absolute intimidation. Matt and Red tried schooching up their chairs even closer to the poor boy, who now had his knees tucked up next to his chest, as if physically protecting himself would also shield him from the psychological onslaught he was no doubt about to go through.

It was at this point that Tom noticed that Red had his stolen laptop in hand, something he must've set in the chair prior to his arrival. Red was typing away at his new toy, not saying anything, every second stretching on like a goddamn eternity in Tom's mind.

"So," started Red, "you like feet, don't you Tom?"

Tom's face went red with embarrassment. "Well, I ... I mean, sure, I guess I ..."

"You want to fuckin' cum on my toes, don't you?" shouted Matt, somewhat angrily.

"You get off on guys socks, don't you?" added Dave. "How much would you pay to take home these socks I've been wearing all damn day, Tom?"

"I, well ..." Tom was stammering out a response, unsure of what to say.

"Nah nah nah," said Red, dismissively, "let's not tease him too much. We have to break his spirit first and then we can have our fun. Got it?"

"Yup," said Dave & Matt in unison.

"Now," Red started, a great deal of regality in his voice, "I got to say, Tom, that stealing your laptop was one of my favorite things to happen to me this year. I mean, I do it sometimes, 'cos you'd be surprised how much a nerdboy will pay to get his computer back. It's not even the quick cash that I find exhilarating. It's the fact that I fuckin' steal some guys' laptop, and once I alert him to the fact I have it, he *doesn't* go to the campus police or the actual police at all. He just does what I say. You know what that tells me, Tom? It tells me that he is a submissive little boy, one that actually wants to be dominated, whether or not he knows it. How do I know? Because by paying me the money to give him his goddamn computer back, he's consenting to the notion that I have his hard drive and I'm selling it back to him for a price. He's consenting to domination, to me being better than him. He views my demands as normal, as reasonable, or otherwise he'd be on the phone with whatever authority figure he could find. You gotta understand something here, boy: there are two types of people in this world. There are subs and there are doms, and say 'switch' all you like but you were meant to only be one. You will either serve or be served, and let me tell you, all three of us are meant to be served. So weird, too: we don't have to do anything and yet you subs just go all crazy over trying to win our approval!"

"You're not just a bitch," interjected Matt, "you're *our* bitch!"

"That's right," Red noted, "and I gotta say, I've messed around with the minds of plenty gayboys in my time, but this -- this is different." Tom could see Red scrolling through something on his computer. "I mean, you've written documents detailing how you got a fuckin' foot fetish, dude. You got confessions about how much you hate being tickled in here. This isn't just a journal, Tom, these are fuckin' letters that you've written. I don't know if they're to help you feel 'at ease' with your sick fetish or what, but man, you obviously must crave some sort of public humiliation, don't you?"

"I ..." Tom stammered out.

"It's almost like you wanted to be caught, isn't it?" Dave chimed in.

"No, I ..." Tom started, flustered.

"Well here's the deal," Red said. "if you want your dirty little computer back, you got to do one thing for us."

Tom's eyebrow arched a bit, curious.

"What is it?" Tom asked.

"You have to sign a contract," Red said. A pregnant pause filled the room. The horror, the mere notion of an actual binding agreement of some sort was absolutely terrifying to young Tom. "Dave, would you be so kind?"

"Absolutely, boss!" Dave jumped out of the sofa with a great deal of enthusiasm, no doubt excited for the prospect at hand. He ran upstairs, leaving Tom simply to look at the two sandaled men that sat before him.

"Come over here and suck 'em!" shouted Matt, appropo of nothing, wiggling his tan toes in those cheap flips. "I know you want to!" Tom simply averted his gaze from Matt's general direction, trying to simply look as small as possible, secretly hoping to disappear. Before Red even got a chance to say anything, the pounding sounds of Dave galloping down the stairs could be heard, and soon Dave was in the main room, handing sheets of paper to the other guys and, finally, one for Tom.

"Here you go, boy," Dave said to Tom, sneering as he returned to the same reclined position he had before on the couch.

"Now," Red started, "you are to read it. In full."

Tom could feel himself sweating. Yet against all odds, he found a way to look at the contract that laid out before him. It read as follows:

TOM'S CONTRACT

I, heretofore to be known as Tom the Footlicker, accept the following terms in exchange for one (1) laptop, which formerly was in my personal possession. This contract extends out to the core members of the TKL Frat, Red, Matt, Dave, and Bobby (heretofore known as his Masters), along with anyone else those four deem worthy of Tom the Footlicker's services.

1.   Tom the Footlicker will hereby address his Masters as "Sir" at all times.

2.   Tom the Footlicker will regularly service the feet of his Masters, but only at times they deem acceptable. Service will include, but not be limited to: sucking on the toes, licking the soles, sniffing the feet for as long as necessary, licking the tops of the feet, thanking his Masters for their feet, complimenting his Masters' feet as frequently as possible.

3.   Tom the Footlicker will not be allowed to even touch his own dick until directed to by his Masters. The same goes for cumming as well.

4.   Furthermore, Tom the
Footlicker will obey every order
his Masters give him, even if it's
outside the scope of Tom the
Footlicker's standard footlicking
services.

5.   Tom the Footlicker will thank
his Masters for their generosity
and kindness whenever is
appropriate.

6.   Tom the Footlicker will make
immediate arrangements to live with
his Masters until further notice.

7.   Tom the Footlicker will not
cry or complain about a task his
Masters have ordered him to carry
out, be it laundry, homework,
serving as the subject of
humiliating photos or otherwise.
Failure to do so will result in
punishment.

8.   Tom the Footlicker will answer
any question his Masters ask of
him, regardless of how personal or
humiliating it may be.

9.   Tom the Footlicker will not
discuss his arrangement with his
Masters unless explicitly directed
by his Masters.

10. Tom the Footlicker will also
service anyone else, member of the
Frat or otherwise, that his Masters
dictate is worth serving. Any other

member may also exploit the
services of Tom the Footlicker
without direct consent of the
Masters so long as it doesn't
interfere with the Masters'
directives.

11. Tom the Footlicker
acknowledges that any property of
his that his Masters' desire will
immediately become the property of
his Masters.

Failure to do any of the above,
whether it be outright refusal of a
request, failure to complete a
task, or failure to complete a task
upon a Masters' specified
timeframe, will result in immediate
punishment. Punishment is up to the
Masters in question, but may or may
not be limited to public
humiliation, forced chastity,
extreme tickle torture, or the
mailing of documents relating to
Tom the Footlicker's fetish to
people that the Masters deem worthy
of informing.

Tom the Footlicker agrees to all
the above via the signature
provided below.

A line with a date was right below that, empty, blank, and waiting
for Tom's definitive signature.

Tom just sat there, flabbergasted. He couldn't believe what he just
read. It was absolutely terrifying the sheer scope and breadth of what
was before him. He wanted to tear it up and grab the laptop and

make a break for it ... but he knew better than that. As he quickly re-read it, just to make sure he got every humiliating detail in his mind, Tom began to feel something that he hated: a stirring. He was already half-erect by the time he had finished reading the document's final lines. As much as this was the single most degrading experience of his entire life, he had never had his fetish presented, manipulated, or otherwise even remotely *thought of* in such a provocative way. Tom's fight or flight response was definitely set to the latter, but given the temptation that laid out here before him, the coda being the absolute perfection of Red's exposed, powerful toes, Tom simply remained, still on the floor, awaiting to hear the frightening details of what his new life was going to be like.

"So," started Red, "what do you say there, boy?"

Tom was thinking long and hard about how to respond. He decided to not agree or disagree to anything, but simply try to slowly change the subject as much as he could.

"So ... I get my laptop back?"

"Yes!" exclaimed Red, "I'll give it back to you *right now* ... after we have a reading, of course. You ready, boys?"

"Got it ready," said Dave, who was looking at something on his smartphone.

"Same here," said Matt, who was also looking at his.

"OK, here we go," started Red, smiling. "Here I was, right in the middle of Matt's frat house ..."

Oh dear god -- they were reading the letter that he wrote in the library last night to Matt! And across all their smartphones, no less! FUCK.

"... and his dirty feet looked so strong in those sandals," Red continued. "He probably didn't think much of it, but seeing those toes move and wiggle on their own was enough to give me a powerful erection."

"What's more," started Dave, reading from his phone but picking up exactly where Red left off, "was the fact that he seemed to be amused, this hypersexual figure of hetero dominance so utterly bemused by a creature -- no, a thing -- that was so powerfully and sexually obsessed with something as simple as his naked toes."

"The creature crawled up to where Matt was sitting," continued Matt, reading on in his very meta moment, "at which point Matt barked out some orders: 'That's right bitch, sniff it. You love the smell of my feet, don't you? You little foot freak. Show me what a fuckin' freak you are.'"

The boys paused as Tom did everything he could to prevent himself from trembling, all of his innermost secrets being read aloud by the boys he fantasized about. Red obviously must've forwarded the email out to everyone or shared the contents of his hard drive on some sort of cloud service, but either way, this little demonstration proved that giving back the laptop was a moot point: Tom's new Masters already had the material that was on it, and they could freely share it with whomever they so desired.

"Well what are you waiting for?" Matt hollered. "Show me what a goddamn freak you are by pleasuring the bottoms of my feet, OK?"

"Now wait wait wait," chimed in David in a very relaxed tone, "let's not go too crazy. I mean, he has yet to actually sign it."

"You're right," noted Red. "Dave, you got a pen for the freak?"

Dave pulled one out of his left jeans pocket, "Right here, my man. Hey boy: take this." He lightly poked Tom in the shoulder with it.

"You better sign it now just to get it over with," Red chirped.

"Yeah, 'cos my feet need to be fuckin' licked over here!" shouted Matt, again.

"Do it!" screamed Dave.

All in all, Tom's head was a blur right now, all this noise and confusion proving to be a poor mix with his humiliating horniness. This all seemed so extreme, so diabolical, the whole thing coming across as some surreal sexual nightmare; there was no way this could be happening in real life right now! Yet as Tom's gaze sauntered the room, seeing Dave's stern smirk, Matt's almost maniacal gaze, and Red's assured look of confidence and dominance, there was nothing Tom could do.

Tom placed the contract on the hardwood floor, used Dave's pen, and almost involuntarily began to to sign the contract, adding today's date at the end as well. With the pen finally lifted from paper, Tom felt a great sinking in his spirit: there was absolutely no turning back now.

"Welcome to Hell, bitch," Red said, smirking. "Dave, rush that over to Bobby and have him digitally scan it for us, would you?"

"With pleasure, my liege!" said Dave, jumping up and snatching the signed contract away from Tom, soon heading off down one hallway of the Frat. A heavy pause hung over the room, Tom frightened to the core as he had no idea what he was going to do next.

"Get over here and suck my feet!" Matt yelled, growing increasingly fervent with each shout.

"No no no," Red interjected, now reclining back in his comfy chair to the point where the leg rest pulled out from under it, leaving his sandaled feet dangling off the end. "I get the boy first, having written the contract. Besides, Matt, I know when you get your turn with him, you ain't gonna show him no mercy."

"You got that right!" Matt hollered back.

"So Tom," Red started, looking at the boy between his reclined legs, "I'm gonna go easy on you. I want you to suck my toes. Right now."

"I ... what?" Tom said, understanding the task but having a hard time fully articulating that it was happening.

"It starting?" said Dave, returning to the room, plopping himself on the couch once again.

"Yes it is," Red said, wiggling his feet, the flip-flops shaking from the toe-holds. "Do what you've always wanted to and suck my toes."

As much as he wanted to have a spine and defy the terrifying reality of his situation, Tom couldn't resist any longer: he leaned forward, himself on all fours now, and crawled right over to where Red's feet were propped up, looking at the worn bottom's of the frat king's sandals. He raised himself up a bit and looked down at the masculine toes that were pointed directly towards his face. For all the roughness that Red seemed to exhibit, the man took damn fine care of his feet, each toenail trimmed and polished, each toe looking pasty, tasty, and clean, an nice bit of pinkness on the tips and undersides of the toes. Just looking at the fuckin' things was making Tom throb uncontrollably. He closed his eyes for a moment, bid farewell to the life he once knew, and dove in.

Tom's mouth descended down and began sucking on Red's big left toe, even though the sandal was still on. With the lip of the sandal pressing into his neck, there was only so much movement that Tom was able to achieve, but boy howdy: wrapping his mouth around that toe, the flood of flavors that came rushing through were unlike anything he had ever experienced. It was tangy and manly and all sorts of indescribable wonderful. Tom felt a twitch in his pants -- this was what he was craving. His tongue stretched out a bit, and began trying to lick the undersides of Red's big toe, and in the process the bottom of his tongue dragged across the sweatblackened toe shape imprinted on Red's sandal, and the flavors just grew that much stronger. A symphony of slave taste were in Tom's mouth right now, and he could barely stand it.

"Shit!" exclaimed Red.

"What is it?" asked Dave.

"Dude, guys ... you gotta experience this. It feels ... fuckin' great!" Red pressed Tom's face back a bit with the bottom of his sandal. "Take it off with your teeth," he ordered. Without hesitation, Tom bit down on the front lip of Red's flip-flop and removed it from his Master's toehold.

"Stop right there!" Matt exclaimed. Both Red and Tom, the latter with a sandal hanging from his teeth, turned to face Matt. A bright flash could be seen, along with a camera snapping sound. Matt just got this image captured on his phone.

"Ooh, good idea!" Dave said. "We need to document *every* single step of this process."

"Why don't you take your shoes off, Dave?" Red asked.

"I dunno -- I was kinda hoping our new houseslave could take care of that task for me," Dave replied.

"Well first thing's first," Red said, "the boy's only touched *one* of my feet, and he hasn't even gone all the way." Red turned to lock eyes with Tom, sandal still in his mouth, and quietly gave him the most terrifying order Tom had ever heard in his life, much less in the fetish fictions he so frequently read: "I want you to fuckin' *embarrass* yourself on my feet right now."

Tom's horny lizardbrain needed no further instruction. The sandal was dropped to the floor and Tom's face went flying into Red's thick, meaty sole, Tom inhaling so deep that everyone in the room could hear the sound of his lungs filling up with toescent. Tom drug his nose up and down the crescent moon of footflesh that was Red's arches, absorbing every smell that could be sniffed. A warmth emanated in Tom's feeble skull, that smell seeping deep down into his subconscious, making his marker-red boner start to pulse just a little more intensely, everything feeling so *good*, everything feeling so *right*.

In fact, as loathe as he was to admit it, Tom had never been happier than he was right now at this instant. All he was smelling was feet. All he was tasting was feet. All he was seeing was feet. All he was thinking about was feet. His cock was turning into a precum faucet at the realization that this was his new reality, his temptation and desire for feet being one of the most extreme and powerful forces he had ever experienced in his life. It was great. It was good. It was ... everything he ever wanted, all summed up in one insurmountable sensation that just so happened to be coursing through his entire body right now.

Of course, being awash in his lust for all things masculine and bearing five toes, Tom somehow failed to notice that he had already taken off Red's other sandal, had licked the tops of the feet until there was a slick sheen of saliva over them, and was currently licking the base of Red's toes on both feet, alternating left and right, left and right, licking and licking and licking like a horse at a goddamn salt lick. Finally, after a furious explosion of desire, Tom could feel his jaw starting to hurt from all this commotion, his mouth having outstretched as far as it can time and time again to try and inhale his new master's powerful toes. He leaned back a bit, just staring at the bare feet that were now doused in his submissive slobber.

Tom looked to his left and could see Dave with his mouth slightly agape, the glanced right to see Matt looking on with wild intensity. Red, meanwhile, had the dumbest of grins on his face, staring at Tom with great intent.

"Dude," he said, "that felt fucking awesome as hell."

"You should've seen him," Dave said, "he was a fucking demon down there. He was *totally* getting into it."

"He's probably harder than a statue down there," Matt noted.

"Oh there's no doubt about that," Red said. "Why don't you unzip your pants and show us the boner you have for my feet, slave?"

Tom immediately got squeamish again. "Please Red, no!" Tom

shouted. "Please don't make me do that."

"Ha ha," Matt chuckled, "he's so embarrassed by how hard that got him. C'mon boy: you signed the contract, so when I say show me your boner, I want to see your fuckin' boner!"

"Yeah, show us!" shouted Dave.

All Tom could do was helplessly look up to Red in hopes of some/any sort of mercy.

"Please don't make me do it, Red," Tom whimpered.

"He didn't call you Sir," Dave noted.

"And he's refusing your order," added Matt.

"You're right," said Red. "I don't think the Footlicker understands the severity of the situation he's in."

"I don't think he does," Dave chimed in. "I think he needs to be punished."

"Capital idea, ol' chum!" said Matt, layering on the sarcasm.

"So what do you think we should do?" asked Red, his toes still wet from Tom's lickings.

"Oh slaveboy," asked Dave, looking at the quiet, almost-trembling Tom, "tell me, what's your roommate's name?"

A flash of panic went through Tom's brain. "I ... I ..."

"Does he stammer every goddamn time we ask him a question?" asked Matt, walking over to where Tom was, his dirty blue flip-flops slapping his heels as he went along. "Answer the question, Footlicker!"

"I can't just ... I ..." was all Tom could get out.

Matt stood there, looking down at Tom, still kneeling on the floor. "Tops of my toes. Your tongue. Right fuckin' now."

Tom, scared, complied, leaning over so his face was just barely hovering over Matt's toes, and christ did they look tasty. The light tan nature of his skin really made the silver of his toenails pop aesthetically, thereby making the entire package something that he couldn't resist.

Tom extended out his tongue, and began sliding it in-between the ring and pinky toe of Matt's right foot. As he did so, Matt lifted up his other sandaled foot and pressed down on the top of Tom's head, pressing Tom's face into the top of Matt's foot harder than ever before.

"Keep licking," Matt said, and despite the pressure on his head, Tom continued to do so, lightly worming his moist tongueworm in-between every toegap there was, and -- just like Red -- also getting some toetaste that had been baked into these flips from years of use. Tom could out of the corner of his eye see Dave, again, using his phone to film some of this. Despite the pressure, Tom's level of arousal was frustratingly constant.

"Tell us the name," Matt said.

Awash with pleasure, Tom couldn't resist any more. "Theron!" he said, before immediately going back to his toelicking duties.

"That's right!" Red exclaimed. "I think I knew that."

Matt let the pressure off of Tom's head and took a few steps back, leaving Tom on all fours, his Masters staring at him with great interest. Red had whipped out the laptop again, and was typing away at it.

"Ah, here we go!" Red said. "*Lusting for the Roommate.* This is a letter you wrote to your buddy Theron, isn't it?"

Tom's brain went into a frenzy. "Oh god no!" he shouted. "Please!"

"Please what?" asked Red, coyly.

"Please ..." Tom started, "Sir."

"There we go," started Red, "that's much, much, much better. That's how you should always be addressing us."

The typing of the computer continued as he spoke: "You know Footlicker, you did literally just sign a contract ensuring that you're going to be servicing us for many moons to come, and all we asked for in return for offering you the hottest pairs of mantoes you've ever seen is your obedience. We think we've been very fair with what we drew up, especially given your very specific set of desires, but failure to not show us your leaking footboner, failure to call me Sir -- these are offenses that we don't take lightly. As such, there will be punishments, as outlined in the contract, and trust me, between me and Matt and Dave here, we fuckin' *love* dolling out punishments, so any excuse you give us to do one is just a tiny little gift in and of itself. As such, I'm going to go light on you this one time here, Tom. The great thing about a campus-wide intranet is the fact that I can pull up the email of any student or teacher just by typing in the first few letters in their name and picking out the rest from the autofill. Thus, yeah, here we go -- we got Theron's email right there. I'm going to attach your little story to this email, and I'm going to ..."

"Fuck no please sir!" Tom blurted out.

"... click send." A little electronic "ding" sound emitted from the laptop, and it was a sound that Tom knew full well meant an email had been sent. Tom was flustered in disbelief.

"You didn't," Tom said.

"Oh, I did!" exclaimed Red. "And what's worse is that there are tons and tons and tons of letters here, Tom. We don't need to gather any incriminating evidence on you here 'cos you so graciously provided so much of it to us. We can send out emails to every single one of these addressees. Maybe we'll get you to tell us your Facebook password and post some stuff there. In fact, maybe we'll just tickle it out of you, 'cos you seem to really fuckin' hate being tickled, don't you, Tom?"

"Well, I ..." Tom started before trailing off again.

"Exactly," noted Red. "Matt just got a photo of you with my fuckin' sandal hangin' from your teeth, and Dave just got a video of you worshiping while in a sandal sandwich, so even if we didn't have those letters, don't you worry: we'll be building up our own mountains of humiliation to use against you in the weeks and months to come." Red looked at Tom with devilish eyes. "Boy, you have *no* fuckin' clue how much shit you're in. This isn't stuff to embarrass you in front of your classmates -- we're going to use this against you for the rest of your known life."

Tom was having a hard time processing all that was being presented to him right now. I mean, college jocks playing a prank is one thing, but to really use him? For the rest of his life? Tom wanted to do a lot of things with his life. He was studying to be a historian, not to be some dumb sex slave for a bunch of dumb jocks! Yet, twisted as it was, Tom still had that part of him that was forcing him to admit that he had fantasized about scenarios like this far too often, frequently running really dark tales of domination through nothing but the manipulation of his raging male foot fetish through his mind again and again and again. Now, here he was, in a real life scenario, and he was genuinely scared and intimidated. The reality of this scenario right now was so overwhelming it deeply terrified him. It would be hours before Tom's mind would be able to wrap his head around the fact that he *actually* signed that contract willingly. Now, here he was, staring down at his own fantasies, and he could see just how powerful, potent, and overwhelming they truly were.

A ding went off, and this time it wasn't from the computer. Everyone looked around.

"What was that?" asked Dave.

"That, um ... that was my phone," said Tom.

"What is it?" asked Matt.

Tom unlocked his phone and could see a text message. The little preview screen told him all he needed to know, and his heart sank.

"It's a text from Theron," Tom said, sadly.

"What's he asking?" asked Matt.

"He ... he wants to know if everything is OK."

"Perfect!" declared Red. "This is a great opportunity for everyone. You know how slaveboy here has to live with us now, right?"

"Right!" chimed Dave.

"Then it's obvious that the Footlicker has to gather his belongings that he needs before we put him in Bobby's room. So, let's make this easy: since his roommate is wondering what the fuck that email was that he just received, why not have the two confront each other?"

"Capital idea!" cried Matt.

"Stop saying that!" Red barked at Matt. "It's stupid. Now, Footlicker, you are to go to your dorm room, gather the necessary materials you need to live here -- and *only* the necessary, as we don't need your posters and shit -- and then report promptly over this house in exactly one hour or we're going to send off another email to someone you don't want us to email. Is that clear?"

"Yes, Sir," said Tom, completely in autoresponse mode right now.

"Well hop to it!" ordered Red.

Tom stood up from the floor, having not stood for a very long time. Looking around, all he could see was his captors staring at him, eyes free of sympathy. Tom turned around to the front door of the frat house, opened it, and--

"Wait a second!" hollered Dave. "I got one more task for you, slave."

"What ... what's that, Sir?"

"When you get over to your room, at some point, you *have* to ask Theron for the opportunity to lick his feet."

"Ooh, I like that!" said Red.

"I wanna hear all about it when you get back," said Dave. "Every. Humiliating. Detail."

"Yes ... Sir," trembled Tom.

And with that, he closed the door behind him, the crisp air of the night whipping him into a state of hyper-consciousness. The night sky seemed to be the darkest he had ever seen it, making the campus streetlamps glow all the brighter. Tom put his hand near his head, trying his best to grasp a hold of what was really real, but right now every single moment of foothumilation he had experienced was seared into his brain, and his mind was rapidly replaying them over and over and over and over again. At the very least, he didn't have to show his footboner, even if he had to do things that were far, far worse.

Taking a deep breath in, Tom began walking back to his dorm room, the reality of what he was going to have to confront with Theron growing with every step. Tom's heart started racing. As scared as he was to meet his captors, something about confronting his roommate and friend over something so personal was even worse. All Tom knew was that even with the night not being over, he was already a completely changed man.

CHAPTER THREE: Confessions

The hallway his room was in never seemed more foreign-looking than right now. Maybe it was the fact that for once Tom felt like he was entering an intimidating situation instead of the room he usually called "home" -- or maybe his mind was taking note that this may very well be the last time he ever actually sees it. Either way, the yellow, dry lamps overhead painted the hallway in a very different light than what he was used to, although deep down he knew this is how it always looked.

Coming to his door, Tom took a deep breath in. It truly was his now-or-never moment. He placed his sweaty palm on the knob, twisted it and entered.

The scene couldn't be more torturous: the room was dark, the TV being the only thing that was providing any source of light, and there was red-headed Theron, feet propped up on that milk crate again, his bare soles perfectly illuminated in that blue haze, and dear christ did they look phenomenal. The soles, the curve of the toes, the pale undersides of each toe, the tip of each toe looking like a flesh orb that cried out for a mouth to suck on it ...

"There you are," said Theron, turning off the TV and turning on a nearby lamp, now making the room glow with a burnt orange hue, Tom now able to see a half-full beer bottle in Theron's hand.

"Yeah, I just came to get some stuff, Theron. I'm probably gonna be sleeping elsewhere for a bit," said Tom, not even making eye-contact with his roommate as he started gathering some basic things: toiletries, an alarm clock, a few changes of clothes. All putting it into the one duffel bag he had just pulled out of his closet.

"Um, why are you sleeping elsewhere?" asked Theron, walking over to Tom's side of the room, still barefoot, which is something Tom tried to avert his gaze from.

"I just ... this is something I got to do. This is ... it's hard to explain," Tom uttered.

"Try me," said Theron, sitting down in Tom's desk chair and taking another swig of his beer. "I can guarantee you that I've probably heard stranger."

"No," started Tom, continuing to pack, "I just ... it's nothing against you, Theron. Nothing against you *at all*. In fact, you've been great. Just phenomenal, even. People would be lucky to have you as a roommate."

"Same to you, cowboy," Theron said, "but there's something you're not telling me. In fact, I'm gonna guess that there are *several* somethings you're not telling me."

"Yeah," said Tom, zipping up the last of his necessaries, "but it's probably for the best."

"Well, you can tell me one thing at least, Tom: what was up with that email that I got?"

Tom was terrible at playing coy, but tried anyways. "Um, what email, Theron?"

"Um, the one from an address that wasn't on campus, but contained a document titled *Lusting for the Roommate*, with your name listed as the author. Do you know anything about this?"

"Um ..." Tom was making the pauses deliberate, trying to buy as much time as he could before he could bolt from there door before answering any more questions. "Ya know, that's a story for another time, I think."

"No, it's a story for right now," Theron said, firmly.

"Sorry, I gotta go," Tom babbled, slinging his weighty duffel bag around his shoulder before bolting for the door.

"Then I'm calling the campus police," Theron said, "for suspicious activity. They consider that a legitimate reason to investigate things now, ya know."

Tom stopped in his tracks.

"Put the duffel bag down," instructed Theron. Tom did so. "Now turn around." Tom did so. "Now sit down." Tom pulled over another milk crate and sat on it.

"Now," started Theron, "what the fuck is going on?"

"I ..." stammered Tom, "it's ... I mean, it's ..."

"Don't get me wrong," Theron interjected, "I love you, but something is up. You're going out at weird hours, you're acting squirrely around personal questions, I'm getting a weird email with this elaborate weird foot fetish fantasy that appears to be written by you -- should I be concerned here? Do we need to report someone or something? Tom, above all else, don't forget that I'm your friend, and *you can trust me*."

A long pause hung over the two young men. Tom knew he wasn't in a right state of mind to be talking about anything, much less making big decisions about things. All that was in his brain right now was whether or not he should tell Theron everything. He knew full well that Theron was a very responsible guy, and also not someone to fully fuck with either. His kindness sometimes got the better of him, but he was fiercely loyal to his friends. Theron was Tom's "Get Out of Jail Free" card, consequences be damned.

Even with salvation taking the form of a burly, scruffy young man who was currently barefoot and surprisingly desirous to Tom, there was a little voice in the back of Tom's head that he hated. A voice that was rational in a different way. A voice that reminded him of the contract, one that he willingly signed, one that said that even if Theron was able to get authorities involved, Red and the rest of the guys would absolutely be able to dominate his life and humiliate him for years down the line. This was the voice that reminded him that despite Theron's best intentions, there was nothing he could do. It was the same voice that reminded him of the one order that he had yet to carry out ...

"Theron," Tom started through nervous lips, "I wanna lick the soles of your feet."

Silence draped the room, as Theron stared directly at his roommate, no emotion visible in his eyes.

"I'm sorry," Theron started, shaking his head as if trying to shake the weird fever-dream that this conversation had become, "... you want to what?"

Tom could feel the words starting to gain power as they emerged from his mouth: "Theron, I have ... a gigantic fucking male foot fetish. It is ... like ... so enormous I can barely articulate the power it has over me."

"So, that letter I was emailed," Theron said, approaching his sentences cautiously, "that was real?"

"Yes," Tom said, gutted but powering through, "that was very, very real. I really don't expect you to understand it at all, because, really, why should you? I take it you've had absolutely no sexual interactions with a man, right?"

"Um, yes, that's *very* correct," Theron said.

Tom felt a weird bit of confidence rise inside of him as he continued speaking: "Well, there are butt guys and there are boob guys and then there are some people into some freaky stuff. Mine is fairly innocuous: I'm just into guys' feet. I think they are truly fucking sexy, and some of the sexiest things to ever exist on this planet. I couldn't tell you why, necessarily, but there's a ... I dunno, a weird kind of intimacy that is experienced when someone goes barefoot around you. It's a part of their body they don't have to show you but invariably they decide when you should see it. Plus, seriously, the fucking shape of toes, especially the undersides -- it's ... irresistible."

Tom stopped for a second to gather where Theron was in this conversation, and Theron was doing the best job he could to not appear completely dumbfounded by what he was hearing. Theron took a few false-starts in speaking before he could finally articulate something.

"Well, um ... cool, I guess? I mean, this doesn't explain why you suddenly got to move out or--"

"Theron," Tom interjected, "it's a long fucking story and I don't really have the time right now, so I got to know -- and keep in mind it doesn't actually matter what you decide -- but would you mind indulging me this one time by letting me lick the soles of your feet? I swear, this is the only time I could ever see myself actually asking."

Theron appeared genuinely baffled by the request. He shook his head back and forth again, trying to fully assess the situation that had been presented to him. He stared directly into Tom's eager eyes, and was flustered once more. He stared again, looked down at this bottle in hand, took a swig of it, and still shaking his head in a doubting fashion, spoke directly to Tom: "Man, you couldn't make this shit up even if you tried."

Theron set his beer bottle on their carpeted floor.

"I mean ... OK," Theron said, "but, like, how does this work?"

A gigantic smile grew across Tom's face, and he did the best he could to conceal it, lest he look like a greedy footpig (even though he knew full well that that's exactly what he was). Tom stood and moved the milk crate he was sitting on and placed it in front of where Theron was sitting.

"OK," Tom started, "prop your feet right on here." Theron did so, his glorious, manly soles and toes staring right back at him.

"For the record, this is really damn weird," Theron said, taking another swig from his beer.

"I know, I know," Tom said, kneeling down in front of the milk crate and, thereby, the feet he had fantasized about licking for oh so long. "Why don't you just close your eyes? I think that might make this go easier for you."

"Whatever," Theron said, taking one last swig of the beer before closing his eyes and tilting his head back. "Do your worst."

Tom needed no more incentive than that. Tom crawled up to Theron's feet, looked up at them, and felt all sorts of tingles course through his system. There was the sheer sexual thrill of it all, the adrenaline that was pumping due to the fact that he wasn't entirely sure when Theron would change his mind, and that added feeling in the back of his head that was alerting him to the fact that he was doing something genuinely naughty, all sealed with the icing of the cake: he had fantasized about doing terrible things to Theron's feet for years.

He first brought his noes up to the base of Theron's toes and inhaled. God, that pungent, powerful odor sent shivers down Tom's spine. He suddenly became submissive, turned on, and empowered all at once. Theron could be the world's best footdom if only he knew how powerful his goddamn feet truly were. Tom took another sniff just to make sure, and just as before, he was overwhelmed with the power that Theron's feet radiated. Theron may very well be a solid candidate for out-and-out Footgod. Shame this was only going to be a one-time thing, Tom dreaded.

Tom raised a bit and craned his head downward, getting a perfect view of the tops of Theron's slightly hairy toes. It was a goddamn visual feast right there. Tom fully acknowledged the powerful footboner that was swelling inside of him, pressing hard against the front of his pants, that sensitive cockhead scraping against the front of his boxer fabric and growing increasingly damp with beads of precum that were slowly leaking out of him. Swelling with horniness, Tom's mouth slowly descended, and casually engulfed the pinky, ring, and middle toes on Theron's right foot. His mouth sealed around them, forming a light suction, and Tom's mouth began slowly extracting as much flavor as he could.

"Oh my," Theron said, head still leaning back and eyes still closed, "this feels ... um ... different."

"I know," said Tom with a grin, mouth stuffed with Therontoes. Tom began moving over to Theron's other foot, tongue slowly working its way in-between each little toegap, relishing the flavor. When he got to Theron's big right toe, he devoted his entire mouth to it, encompassing the base with his moist lips and then slowly, sensuously sucking up and down, up and down, up and down, each iteration slower than the last. Tom could swear he heard slight groanings coming from Theron, but they were very quiet. Tom was nonetheless pleased by this.

After paying some good attention to his left toes as well, Tom then went in and placed his face right near Theron's left heel. Tom took out his tongue, and the tip touched the center of Theron's heel. Tom then drew his face closer, so that his tongue was laid flat against the entirety of the heel. With that, Tom slowly dragged his tongue up, taking in as much of the flavor as he could, leaving a trail of his mouthjuice behind him as he went. The closer he got to Theron's toes, Theron started trying to suppress some giggles.

"Dude," he said, "that tickles!"

"It's OK," Tom said back, smiling, "I'll go easy on you."

Tom started again at the heel, dragging the tongue up once more, this time spending more time on Theron's instep as he worked that horny tongue up to the toes. Tom repeated this again on Theron's right foot twice, his dick tingling in approval the second time out. Tom then worked his way back to Theron's toes, each one a delicious little meat candy that melts in your mouth, not in your hands. Tom selfishly began slurping his roommates toes again and again, the occasional giggle spurting out of Theron's mouth, pleasing Tom to no end.

Finally, with the roof of his mouth now flavored with Theronfoot, Tom disengaged and simply stared at the feet he had worshiped, now covered in a nice glaze of saliva, glistening as it reflected the dull orange lamp that was illuminating the room. That image right then and there seared itself into Tom's brain. This was a mental postcard he'd refer back to time and time and time again. This was incredible. This was amazing. This is what Tom had always wanted.

That being said, he did fear whatever questions Theron would inevitably have after this worship session was over. Not wanting his break from toe-sucking to go on too long, Tom quietly got the strap of the duffel bag around his shoulder and looked up at Theron, grateful his eyes were still closed.

"Don't open your eyes just yet -- I want to grab something for you. I think you're going to really like it."

"Um, OK," Theron said, laid out there with eyes closed and his feet moist, lost in some sort of accidental bliss. Tom picked up the duffel bag and made his way to the door, quietly closing it behind him. He then simply started going down the stairs and out the front entrance, beelining straight for the TKL frat house. In truth, Tom felt really guilty about just leaving his roommate there with his toes soaked in saliva and an infinite amount of questions in his head. However, Tom viewed exiting when he did the only sure-fire way to avoid the brunt of those inquiries. Although he was still panicked over the scenario, Tom was noticeably less nervous than before, and somewhat awash with pride: he just barely sucked on three pairs of mantoes in the past few hours ... and the night wasn't even over yet.

CHAPTER FOUR: Introducing Bobby

"There the fuck you are," Matt said when Tom arrived at the door. "You barely made it in under an hour."

"I know Sir," Tom said, putting his duffel bag down as Matt closed the door behind him. "I was just in the middle of ..."

"I don't give a shit what you were in the middle of," Matt said, "I got toes that need licking right the fuck now." Matt aggressively put his arms on Tom's stomach and upper back and practically threw him to the ground in one quick motion. From here, yes, Tom could very clearly see Matt still wearing those same blue flip-flops from before. "Start lickin'!" he yelled.

Right as Tom began opening his mouth, Red entered the main foyer. "Stop it, Matt," he beckoned.

"Oh c'mon, Red!" Matt protested. "He's ours to use as we please, and he's here to please us. Let me have the little shit do what he does best."

"Not yet," Red said, walking over, "we can't go too hard too quick. Boy needs some positive reinforcement now and then. He made it back here within an hour, he called you Sir: these are all good things." Red glanced down at Tom still on the floor, inches away from both Masters' pair of sandaled feet. "Besides, just wait until the interrogation we put him through. We gotta raise his spirits up before we drag him *all* the way down."

Matt sighed, "You're right. I just wanna fuckin' use him."

"I know," Red said, "but for now, let's get him in his room."

"Oh yeah, he has yet to meet Bobby, doesn't he?" Matt noted.

"I'd say we introduce him here right now, don't you?" Red said, smirking.

"Capital idea!" Matt said, soon turning his gaze towards Tom. "Alright bitch, grab your stuff. You're gonna meet your roommate.

Better be nice ..."

Red and Matt started walking off down a hallway behind the main staircase, and Tom scrambled to stand up and grab his bag, lugging it over his shoulder before hurrying up to follow them. A few feet down, there was a door on the left, and both Red and Matt stood outside of it. Tom schlepped his bag closer to them, and they stood there, grinning.

"Well boy," Red started, "feel lucky that you get one of the most sympathetic people you're going to meet during your ordeal -- and you get to sleep on his floor every goddamn night. Footlicker, meet Bobby."

Tom went in front of the door way and saw a very different kind of room: messy as all get out, one bed, lots of racks of CDs and books. The bed only took up a quarter of the room, and a computer station took up a quarter just opposite of it. That meant there was a whole half of the room covered with fliers, papers, written-in notebooks, a speaker system, used clothes, and a smattering of other things. To call it disorganized would be an understatement.

Yet right there at the computer, in a dark blue hoodie, was Bobby: a scruffy brown beard on his face to offset his nicely-combed head of hair, a slightly smaller stature, blue-jeans and ratty white socks making up for the rest of his dress. Yet when Bobby turned to look at Tom, the Footlicker was immediately struck by Bobby's face: open, bright, and with eyes that were ice-blue in color. Some might call him a bit too schlubby to be dreamy, but Tom was immediately taken with the scruffy young man with a single glance.

"Hey there," Bobby said, lifting his head up in acknowledgment before turning back to the computer he was seated at, a pair of headphones draped around his neck.

"Here's the thing about Bobby," Red started, "he doesn't care for any of this business. He's a very valuable member of our Frat and kind of a technical genius, but he doesn't care for some of the other activities we do here, especially in regards to hopeless little footlickers we have under contract. Now, Bobby is named in the contract you signed, so if he demands you do something, you fucking do it, got it?"

"Got it," Tom said, still ogling Bobby, who was still staring at his computer, disinterested.

"There are a few rules towards this arrangement though," Red stated. "For one, you don't get a bed. You sleep on Bobby's floor. Two, you don't speak to Bobby unless you're spoken to by him. He's already doing us a solid by allowing your little slave body to sleep on his floor. Bobby will graciously report any infractions of these rules directly to us, and I assure you, although Bobby doesn't really care what happens to you, Dave, Matt & I will very much make sure your punishments are carried out to the fullest, OK?"

"And don't sniff my socks," Bobby said, still not looking at Tom.

"Yeah," Red said, "Bobby doesn't really 'get' your weird little fetish, so don't you dare start imposing anything onto him, OK?"

"OK Sir," Tom said.

"Am I missing anything?" Red said, turning to Matt.

"When's your first and last class?" Matt inquired.

"Um, 7am for my first period and my last period gets out at 2:30pm. That's how it goes for most days," Tom said.

"Alright," Red noted, "we usually got classes and maybe practice 'til about 5pm, sometimes 5:30pm. So listen: you will use your time between your last class and the time we get home to do your fuckin' homework or whatever. Once 6pm hits though, you are ours to do as we please with for as long as we please, got it?"

"Yes," said Tom, affirmatively.

"Good. Now go make a place to sleep at on Bobby's floor here and get a good night's rest," Red ordered. "Trust me, you're going to fucking need as much energy as you can tomorrow ..."

"Understood, Sir," answered Tom.

"Later, bitch," said Matt as the two Masters walked off, the sound of those sandal slaps echoing down the hallway, leaving Tom in Bobby's doorway, duffel bag wrapped around his shoulder.

"Will you get in and close the door already? You're letting a draft in," said Bobby, still staring directly at his computer screen.

"Yes Sir," Tom said, getting in and closing the door behind him.

"You can call me Bobby. It's fine."

"Yes Sir," Tom said, catching himself saying "Sir" just on autopilot.

"Whatever," said Bobby, putting his headphones on, "just make a room for yourself on the floor. Oh, and be careful with my stuff."

"Yes Sir," Tom said.

Tom began making his way over to a small clearing in the floor, and began pushing some things aside -- carefully of course -- in order to make a sleeping space. His eyes glanced over the objects he moved as he did so: boxes for headphones and various fruit-based health bars. It was a curious sight, although he took pause when he saw some of those dirty socks that Bobby must have no doubt thrown out without any sort of consideration: socks that were perhaps one day white but were now a milky gray, all from months or years of wear-and-tear or just not having been properly washed. Now from what Tom could tell, Bobby was a hygienic individual, but he was just lazy with other things, like laundry and organizing and all that stuff. Even while pushing piles of stuff out of the way to make a good sleeping space, Bobby didn't turn his head once from his computer to acknowledge the new person living in his room. The boy was intent on something, very smart and sharp, from what Tom could determine -- why would he bother with such a simple task as laundry? It didn't make any sense for him.

Finally having carved out a nice oval-shaped space on Bobby's hardwood floor, Tom got some clothes out of his bag, balled some up into a pillow, pulled out a towel he packed and used it as a blanket. The room was warm enough where it wasn't really going to effect things much, but he was just happy to have a place to sleep.

As he placed his head down, all in the dead silence of the room, the earphones still firmly glued to Bobby's ears, Tom was looking at the black wire-frame shelf that separated him and Bobby sitting at his computer. Through that open-mesh wiring, often used to store DVDs or the like, Tom was actually able to get a pretty decent view of Bobby sitting at his desk. Bobby sat at his computer, face illuminated by his computer screen, and had his right jean-panted leg crossed over his left, basically giving Tom a perfect view of his socked sole. The outline of Bobby's actual foot and toes were visible through the grayer parts of those sweaty socks, but for whatever reason -- be it his exhaustion, his humiliation, the fact that his brain was having the hardest of time believing these past 24 hours were actually real -- but Tom's eyes got lost in those socked feet of Bobby's.

There it was, a powerful male foot, horizontal with the ground, existing, sweating, and simply looking like an object of absolute perfection. The longer Tom stared, the more he noticed Bobby would occasionally wiggle his toes, unconsciously of course, and Tom could see the movement of each individual toe underneath that perfect white cotton just entice him all the further. While horny lust would just keep him up longer, Tom's body was too worn out by the day's events to do much of anything on the physical front, so Tom's eyes slowly began shutting on their own, Bobby's socked sole being the last thing he saw on this transformative day. "I love feet," Tom quietly thought, before sleep completely overtake his mind, and he drifted off into an exhausted slumber.

+ + +

Tom was awoken by the sharp pinging sounds of an alarm. It wasn't the one on his phone that he set every day to wake up, no. Tom looked around: yes, he did somehow remember to plug his phone into the wall charger he brought with him last night, but as he clicked the button on his phone to light up the screen, he could see it was 5:45AM -- well before he had to go to his first class. His own phone alarm was often for 6:15AM.

It was at that moment that Tom realized his surroundings: he was surrounded by clothes that weren't his own, in a small and dirty dorm room that was ... oh yes, in a frat house. Bobby. That sock-footed wunderkid with the brown beard. It Bobby's alarm clock that was going off. Tom lifted his head and saw there was an old-school radio alarm clock on the floor near the head of his bed. Bobby was nestled under his covers, and Tom watched as Bobby's half-awake arm flopped out of the sheets and swatted at the ground next to his bed, eventually hitting the big ol' snooze button on that alarm clock. The arm quickly retracted back into its resting place, but Tom ... Tom was very much awake at this point. That rush of fear and excitement over all that was happening to him returned, and it returned in a thunderous fashion.

Tom mulled his options as he looked around Bobby's messy room: does he get up and go now? Does he he change? Does he pretend to sleep? For the time being, Tom rested his head on the pile of clothes that he had fashioned into a bit of a pillow. His eyes wide open, Tom could see the first rays of morning sun start pouring through the room. Bobby had the blinds drawn over his room's two windows, but those warm slivers of golden sun were starting to manifest.

Bobby rustled a bit in his bed, and after a moment, went back to some very light snoring. Tom was no fool: he had been in situations like this, and he knew full well that Bobby could pop out into full-consciousness at any point, so as much as his stupid lizard-brain fed him the idea to see if he can get a glimpse (or lick) of Bobby's naked toes through the covers, Tom immediately thought better of it. Red and the other boys painted a very sympathetic picture of Bobby last night, so Tom knew full well that if he had a real emotional "ally" in this, it would be him. Best to let sleeping Bob's lie.

Tom quietly unzipped the duffel bag he brought with him last night and got out a change of clothes, quietly changing and tossing on some deodorant, all in hopes of not waking up Bobby as he quietly half-snored. With his sneakers finally on, Tom picked up his backpack, slung it over his shoulder, and was ready to head out.

At that moment, a not-really-awake Bobby twisted in bed again, and, suddenly, his left foot stuck out a bit from under the covers. Tom's eyes immediately darted to look: and Bobby was still wearing those dusty white socks of his. They went all the way up to his shins normally, but here were a bit loose and crumpled around the ankles. Tom got the sense that Bobby wasn't much of an ankle-socks guy, but could also be very wrong about that as well. Either way, Tom simply made a bee-line for the door. He quietly opened it, but there was a bit of a creak to it. "Great," Tom thought, "now he's going to know if I'm ever entering or leaving." Tom glanced at Bobby's sleeping face -- no movement. He must already be used to the door creak, so Tom wasn't disturbing his sleep in the least. Tom stepped out into the hallway, and closed the door as quietly as he could. The small victories counted at this point.

Tom started heading towards the front door, across the main hardwood gathering room he was so tormented in the night before, but right in the middle of the room was a very thin night stand, and on it, his laptop. Tom's face lighted up with relief, and almost raced over to see his old friend. As he drew closer, Tom saw a giant piece of paper was taped right on top of it:

> "HEY FOOTLICKER! You'll need to do
> your studies, but all your content
> is on our cloud. All. Of. It. See
> you tonight ..."

Tom knew this information already -- this threat was nothing new, and he had already accepted the cruel reality that he was in. However, he viewed the guys giving him back his laptop as a sign of good faith. Against all odds, Tom's heart was bursting with warmth. Even though lingering doubts about his scenario still swirled in his mind, gestures such as this made him realize it wasn't all going to be hopeless and soul-crushing, no. In fact, if he played his cards right, Tom might even have some fun.

Being how it was a solid hour before his next class, Tom decided to grab an actual breakfast, and proceeded to go to the campus cafeteria. He was surprised they were open at 6AM, but then again Tom realized he had never been up earlier enough to take advantage of the cafeteria. He grabbed some cereal and an apple, had his choice of table given how almost no one was in here, and proceeded to open up his laptop to actually maybe catch up on some things before his first class.

His password, mercifully, remained unchanged, but as soon as his homescreen loaded, Tom saw that the guys had decided to creatively change his backdrop to what appeared to be ... a shot of Dave & Matt's soles? The flash was a bit too close so the soles themselves were a bit blurry, but the toes, the outlines, everything else was there, and the flash illuminated just enough of Dave & Matt's smiling, smug faces in the background. As great as their feet were, that's what absolutely killed it for Tom: those faces that indicated they knew exactly how much control they had over their newest frathouse resident. As much as Tom would like to be put off by such deliberate tormenting, it actually had quite the opposite effect on him, and he was ... well, he was starting to feel all the right tingles in all the right places.

Clenching his spoon tightly almost as if telling his brain to get a grip of things, he quickly loaded up his email and proceeded to eat cereal whilst he glanced over all the emails he had missed since this ordeal started. Syllabus for a science class, a few campus-wide alerts about remembering to change your password (which was promptly deleted) -- none of this was new. Then, he came across an email from ... Theron. The subject line was simple: "You OK?" Tom's heart, naturally sank out of guilt over the whole thing, but knew he had to read on no matter what:

> "Hey Tom.
>
> So, yeah, let's not beat around the

bush: last night was pretty weird.
Like, really bizarre. I mean,
things happened that I didn't think
would ever, EVER happen, but the
underlying feeling to all this is
that I'm worried about you. I mean,
you seem kinda sorta confident in
whatever it is that's going on,
but, ya know, I thought we were
friends. I thought you could trust
me with just about anything. You
seem to be confident about where
you're staying and what you're
doing, so, hey, I won't interfere
if you don't want me to. Just know
that no matter what, I'm still your
friend, and there will always be a
bed here for ya.

Seriously man: do what you need to
do but at least let me know that
you're OK, OK? Foot fetish or no, I
got your back.

--Theron."

As if the past two days weren't already emotionally taxing enough,
Theron had to send this. Tom put his spoon down and simply
pressed his face into his hands. It was so, so, so easy for him to get
"lost" in the sheer fantasy indulgence of what was going on, but
Theron was grounding him right now, making him realize that what
was happening was absolutely absurd. Maybe he *should* go to the
campus police about this -- but dammit, he had his laptop back now.
Plus the guys would just go crazy and humiliate him to no end.
Looks like he was just gonna go through with it. But maybe, well--

Tom checked his phone: class started in 10 minutes. Crap. He shut
his laptop and put his tray and bowl away. His mind was awash in
too many thoughts and conflicting emotions to properly think

straight right now. He hustled to class, but his mind was very much elsewhere.

As the day and classes wore on, Tom couldn't help but notice that he couldn't keep focused on a single damn thing. His brain was wandering to a variety of topics: how hot Red's soles were, how guilty he felt about leaving Theron with all the questions that he had, how hard he got simply thinking about Matt demanding that he lick the spaces between his toes again, how he wondered if he should just disappear and never return to the frat house just to avoid any more awkwardness, how badly he wanted to see Bobby's feet without socks on -- it was a roller coaster of emotions.

In fact, Tom was so awash with all these conflicting thoughts that he hadn't even had a chance to notice the fact that he was already done with his classes for the day. He shook his head, as if coming out of some haze, and pulled out his notebook: not a single thing was written down all day. Man, he really couldn't concentrate on shit. Instead, all he could think about was how 6pm was coming along around the corner, and there wasn't much of anything he could do about it. That mixture of fear and excitement swirled around his body, and Tom did what he could to ignore it while buying a quick takeaway meal from the campus cafe before heading back to the TKL frathouse.

By the time he was walking up the steps, it was 3pm: the sun was still out, and everyone crossing the campus sidewalks seemed to be in the usual upbeat college spirits. Even with his laptop now returned to him, Tom walked towards the main entrance with trepidation. He opened the door, and peered inside -- even though this was his new "home," he still felt like a guest more than a resident. No one seemed to be around, at least as far as he could tell. He went through the main hang area and made his way to Bobby's room. He knocked quietly at the door and whispered "Hello?" No response. He opened the door, still creaking, and saw no one was around. He threw his bag down in the oval of space he cleared out for himself and fired up his laptop, opening up his takeaway meal to nibble while he worked.

It was strange: despite the lingering fear over everything that was happening, Tom felt ... strangely at peace here in Bobby's room. He felt like he could concentrate on things, and before long, he managed to actually catch up on some emails and some quiz-work over the course of 90 minutes. Despite his laptop's new background, he still remained remarkably active in his studies, and actually felt pretty good about things.

Tom wiped the last remaining crumbs of pre-packaged sandwich from his mouth and crumpled up his little dine-n-dash meal. He looked to see where Bobby's trash can was, and lo' and behold, it was right near the computer. Tom got up and walked over to it before noticing that it was filled near the brim. No bag liner of course: just a black plastic bin that was filled with papers and tissues and crumpled soda cans. Thinking that he would like to make a good impression with his new roommate, Tom had the novel idea of taking it out to the trash for him. Tom picked the thing up (since it was largely paper-based things, it was pretty darn light) and made a left out of Bobby's door, kind of hoping he'd run into the kitchen.

Indeed, right around this other corner, Tom found the kitchen with a cheap linoleum floor. With the precious few campus parties he's attended in the past, Tom knew that most times the larger dumpsters for buildings such as this were kept out back. The kitchen had a locked wooden door that lead directly out back, and as soon as he opened it, there indeed was the frat's dumpster. Tom opened up the giant lids for it before emptying Bobby's trash bin. "Hey," Tom thought, "I'm doing pretty good for myself."

Tom came back in to the kitchen and locked the door behind him. "Hey Footlicker!" a voice cried out. Tom's had sharply snapped around, panicked. Standing in the doorway to the kitchen was Dave, his face wide with enthusiasm, his ink-dark eyebrows arcing in a way that really highlighted the boyish charms to his face. "What the hell you doing, man?"

"Bobby's trash was full so I thought I'd empty it for him ... Sir."

"Hey, that's some good thinking," started Dave, walking over to him. "I'm thinking that you should probably do that for all your Masters.

Don't you think that's a great idea?"

"Yeah," stammered Tom, "I mean, if it's not too much hassle."

"Oh, it won't be," said Dave, getting uncomfortably close into Tom's personal space, "not at all."

A lingering silence hovered over the two men. Tom was getting more uneasy with each passing second, while Dave simply stared at Tom with his big blue eyes like some sort of shark.

"You didn't compliment me on my shoes, Footlicker," Dave said, somewhat menacingly.

"I'm sorry, I just ... I ..." Tom was at a loss for words.

"Ha," laughed Dave, "I'm just joshin' ya. You're not really a 'shoe' guy, are you?"

"No, Sir," replied Tom.

"You're more of a 'bare feet' guy, ain't ya, Footlicker?" sneered Dave.

"Yes Sir," said Tom. Another silence hovered as Dave just kept staring. "Would ... would you like me to ... service your feet now, Sir?"

"Ha!" laughed Dave, "Oh man, you just make things too easy. No no, you don't have to now. Besides, it's my night with you, and I got a hell of a plan mapped out for you as well."

"It's ... it's *your* night?" asked Tom.

"Oh yeah!" said Dave, backing away towards the kitchen entrance. "Guess we forgot to mention: since it's Wednesday now, each of us get a night to do what we want with you. Tonight's mine, tomorrow's Matt's, and Friday is the day you get to be Red's bitch. Figured we'd all get a chance to totally break you in our own ways. How does that sound, Footlicker?"

"That sounds ... great, Sir," stated Tom, somewhat unsure of himself.

"Oh, but ... *man*, you have no idea what I got in store for you. It's just ... oh man, it's just ... great." Dave seemed more excited the more he talked about it. "Just ... just get ready, dude. You ain't gonna be the same guy by the time I'm done with you."

"Um, OK," said Tom. "Thank you for the heads up, Sir."

"Oh, don't mention it," said Dave, "'cos I doubt you'll be smilin' by the end of it. Tonight's gonna be off the chain, motherfucker!" Dave slapped the kitchen door frame with enthusiasm and then split. Tom took a moment to take this new information, and although he was dreading it a bit -- he honestly was kind of expecting something brutal to happen. After all, with everything he went through last night, Tom realized that that was only his introduction to the boys. Their confidence in what they'll be able to do with their own personal slaveboy was only going to grow was time went on.

Tom went back to his room and put Bobby's now-empty trashcan back in its place. He then got back to his little space near the windows and proceeded to keep on working. Amazingly, despite Dave's lingering threat, Tom was able to get back into a nice work "groove," and soon had another paper outline knocked out. All things considered, today wasn't the worst.

Around 5:15pm or so, that familiar door creak reached Tom's ears and he looked up to see Bobby coming back into his room. Tom contemplated saying "hi" to the boy but decided against it. Bobby took off his backpack and just plopped it next to the chair facing his computer. Without even looking at Tom, Bobby simply sat down and powered his computer back up. Bobby pulled a bottled water out of his backpack and took a swig. As he screwed the cap back on, he looked around a bit.

"Hey, did you take my trash out?" he asked Tom without even looking.

"Yeah," he replied, "I hope that's OK."

"Yeah, no," said Bobby, "that was real nice of you. Thank you."

"Anytime!" Tom said with a bit too much enthusiasm. Bobby turned to look at Tom with an arched eyebrow and then turned back to his computer, tossing on this headphones again to get lost in ... whatever it was that he was doing.

Wow, of all the people he was now surrounded by, Tom himself was wondering why he was trying so hard to impress Bobby, even withing 24 hours of meeting him. Looking at that distinguished brown beard of his, there was just ... something about Bobby that was intriguing. Even though he likely was the "tech genius" who helped get all the embarrassing contents of his hard drive up onto the frat's shared cloud account, there was something weirdly sympathetic about Bobby's demeanor. From his initial interactions, Tom was able to determine that Red was smarter than he let on with his jock appearance, manipulative but understanding; Dave was a bit wild and way overenthusiastic, but strangely Tom didn't feel horrendously threatened by him.

However, Matt, hands down, was the one he feared the most. Matt was like a dog off a leash, apparently uninhibited in his actions and unbridled in terms of his ego. He's the kind of guy that would get what he wanted but would throw an aggressive hissy fit if for some reason he didn't. He was all raging id, unafraid of consequences no matter what they might be, and, most of all, unafraid of how it all tied back to him. Although he was worried about what was going to happen each and every one of those nights, perhaps he was most afraid of his night with Matt, beca--

"Hey, Tom," shouted Bobby.

"Yes?" said Tom, almost completely forgetting where he was being so lost in his thoughts.

"It's 6pm. You're needed up in Dave's room."

"Oh," said Tom, getting up, "well, thanks for letting me know. I guess I'll be seeing you la--"

"No," interrupted Bobby, standing up, "I'm coming with you."

"I thought this was just Dave's night with me," Tom noted.

"It is," said Bobby, "and for his night, he invited all of us and a special guest to witness what was going to happen to you."

Tom gulped. "Special guest?"

"Yes, the one with the camera," said Bobby rather flatly. "Now get goin'. It's time."

Tom was not comfortable with a camera. Not by any means whatsoever. However, as he was learning to come to accept in these scenarios, it's not like he had much of a say in the matter anyways.

CHAPTER FIVE: Lights, Camera, Action

Bobby lead Tom upstairs, which Tom hadn't seen before. In truth, it wasn't anything special: it was a simple hallway with a bunch of doors on either side. The guys' names were on each door, and there were a few frat members that Tom hadn't met yet: Brian H., Johnard, Johnny, Seth M. Tom wasn't surprised by this, really: he just thought it was strange that he's really only seen four guys during his entire time here.

Bobby knocked on Dave's door. "Who is it?" cooed Dave from the inside. "Me with the meat," replied Bobby. "Then you may enter, good sir! J.C.'s just making the final adjustments and we're off!" Dave bellowed in reply.

Bobby opened up Dave's door, and much to Tom's surprise, there were already quite a few people here: Red, Matt, Dave, and a mop-topped young guy who he didn't recognize. His hair was a light brown and currently in a nice swoop formation. That guy was behind a pretty high-grade film camera that was on a tripod. Tom guessed that this was J.C. It was facing the wall adjacent to Dave's doorway, wherein a big white projector screen was placed. In front of the projector screen were three chairs in a bit of a triangle formation, one chair with its back directly to the blank white screen. The rest of the guys were huddled behind Dave's desk, where his computer appeared to be hooked up to the camera. The monitor, of course, was facing away from the entrance, so Tom couldn't really make out what was going on. From what Tom could tell, all of the guys (save J.C.) were wearing shoes.

Dave stepped out from behind the monitor. "Bobby! Footlicker! Good to see you both!" he proclaimed.

"Are you able to access the videos OK?" asked Bobby.

"Oh yes," noted Dave. "Things are going exactly as planned. You wanna help with the zip-ties?"

Bobby sighed, "Yeah, sure, I guess."

"What's wrong there, Bob-o?" asked Dave.

"Bondage just ain't really my thing, much less facilitating it," he sighed.

"Don't worry," said Dave, "but this is my night with the thing-boy, and I really want to make sure he follows through with it all the way to the end." Tom couldn't help but notice that the two were talking about him as if he wasn't even in the room.

"Alright, let's get this over with," said Bobby, grabbing some zip-ties that Dave had pulled out of his jeans pocket.

"Hey, Footlicker!" Dave said, snapping his fingers in Tom's face, "It's your time to shine! Why don't you take off your shoes and pants for me?"

"Um," stammered Tom, flustered again, "like, right here?"

"Oh my god," started Dave, tilting his head up in disbelief, "yes, right fucking here. In front of all these people. Remember, *you* are the one who signed the contract let's not forget."

"OK, it's just, I--"

"Oh, I'm sorry, are you hesitating, Footlicker?" sneered Dave before turning to shout at Matt. "Hey Matty! You want to send another email to his roommate?"

"No no!" shouted Tom, "I'm sorry. Here." With that, Tom started toeing off his sneakers and removed his jeans, leaving him in his shirt, boxers, and white socks.

"Much better," said Dave, rather dramatically. "Now if you'd please, Footlicker, would you sit at that chair in front of the screen with your arms behind it?"

"Yes Sir," whimpered Tom, simply doing as he told.

As he sat down, Bobby came around and went behind the chair, soon binding Tom's arms behind his back with zip-ties. Nervousness was seeping in, as Tom couldn't really go anywhere, as Bobby had looped his wrists through the back posts of this wooden ol' thing he was sitting in. Now immobilized, Tom was noticing that the camera that other guy had was pointed directly at him, no doubt getting his face but also getting his crotch and feet in frame as well. Although there was some light shining on him, he couldn't help but notice the guy operating the camera was standing in cheap green plastic flip-flops, and, no lie, had some very nice toes to look at, well-shaped with the tips of them looking a bit bulbous, and therefore completely juicy and enticing.

"Alright, we ready?" shouted Dave, to which he received murmurs of agreement in response. "Alright, let's do this thing. We rolling, J.C.?"

"We rolling," the cinematographer said, his voice a bit high pitched.

"Then let's get to it! Masks on, everybody."

Tom looked around and saw that everyone there, save this J.C. guy, had on a black ski-mask, and at the same time, they all pulled it over their heads. Tom was *really* fucking worried now.

At that moment, Dave stepped in front of the camera and faced it directly as he spoke, the ski-mask fitting his melon rather nicely: "Dear home viewer, welcome to what will no doubt be known as the world's most intriguing reality show. We're not just going to show you reality, but we're going to show you a reality that rarely gets seen. Tonight, we are going to dive into the mind of an honest-to-god footlicker. His name, of course, is Footlicker."

Dave stepped aside so the camera could focus in on Tom. For whatever reason, Dave stepping away from the rolling camera made all the lights seem brighter, which might also have been an after-effect of his overwhelming sense of worry.

"Say hi to the camera, Footlicker!" Dave said brightly. Tom simply squinted his eyes due to the light and tried to not look at the camera as much as he could. "Aww, it looks like Footlicker is a bit camera shy. Let's try this one more time: say hi to the camera, Footlicker!"

"Hi there," Tom said, quietly, now fidgeting with his zip-tie cuffs more than he was before.

"Aww, would you look at that? He's a natural star!" exclaimed Dave, looking back at the camera again. "And for the next, well, however long this takes, we are going to probe Footlicker's mind, and extract every secret and ugly truth we can from him, all for your viewing pleasure! How does that sound, Footlicker?"

Tom hyper-ventilated for a moment, but quickly said "Sounds great, sir." As scared as he was, Tom knew how it would be more important to play along than it would be to defy orders.

"Great!" said Dave. "Now let's dive in, shall we?" Dave walked over and stood beside the camera -- not in frame -- and stared at his bound young victim. "Now Footlicker," he started, "tell me: what's the most devious thing you've ever done with your foot fetish?"

Tom was a bit flabbergasted. "The ... the most devious thing I've done with my fetish? What do you mean?"

"You know," started Dave, "the one thing you yourself felt super guilty about afterwards."

"I ..." stuttered Tom, "I ... don't ... I don't know. I just ..."

"Oh c'mon," moaned Dave, "you know you got to have some skeletons in your closet. In fact, you better start telling me in the next five seconds, or there's gonna be some rather unpleasant punishment for you. Let's count slowly, shall we? Five ..."

"No, you don't understand," exclaimed Tom, "I just--"

"Four," Dave continued.

"Please! I've actually done some bad things. I mean, I feel like--"

"Three. More specificity, Footlicker."

"I don't wanna name names!" yelled Tom. "I don't want to drag people into this that--"

"Two," continued Dave. "I wanna hear a name, Footlicker."

"OK OK OK OK!" screamed Tom. "His name was Ash! He was a friend of mine. A bit portly, a bit of a stoner. He had these feet that were pudgy and meaty and honestly kind of ... well ..."

"Yes?" coursed Dave.

"... they were ... god, they were sexy," said Tom, resigned to his fate. "They were delicious-looking. I knew he'd never let me have them so ... I took some pictures. I mean, I always take candid photos with my phone when I can, but these ones ... these ones I put online. Just on message boards for other people to see. They also thought they were hot, and it was great. But ... fuck me ... I stole his socks. Back home, I actually still have a few pairs of his dirty socks in zip lock bags. I learned this technique from the founder of Foot Fraternity -- it's a pretty popular website -- wherein you can just spray a little bit of water on them and microwave them in the zip bag for 30 seconds and it kind of reinvigorates the stink. It's ... great. I also stole a sandal of his. A worn shower flip-flop. Cheap. Plastic. You could see his toe-prints worn into them pretty well. They didn't smell as pungent but they were still pretty great to have. So ... yeah. That's what I did with Ash's footwear. I stole it and sniffed it and got off to it."

A pregnant pause filled the room.

"Dude," said Dave, "that's really fucked up. I mean, that's *really* fucked up, man. Holy shit you love feet, don't you?"

Tom's head sagged a bit. "Yes," he resigned, "I do."

"No," continued Dave, mockingly, "but you like *love* love feet. Like, you go fucking crazy over them, don't you?"

"Yes," Tom sighed again. "I do."

"Do you go crazy over *my* feet, Footlicker?"

"I haven't seen yours yet," said Tom.

"Well," said Dave, adjusting himself into a dominant tone, "play your cards right and who knows, you might just get to." He cleared his voice a bit. "Now, onto more serious matters: what happened when you asked your roommate if you could lick his feet?"

Tom's eyes went wide: "No! Please! He has nothing to do with this!"

"Who?" teased Dave, playing with his prey.

"Theron! My roommate!" said Tom, sounding as desperate as ever.

"So, you went back to your room to gather your stuff," started Dave, pacing back and forth across the camera's frame of vision like he was in some courtroom TV show, "and, per the instructions of your newly-minted Masters, you asked him if you could lick the soles of his bare feet, correct?"

Tom bit his lip and simply nodded in agreement.

"And what did he say to that, Footlicker?"

Tom simply continued holding his face in a defiant grimace, not giving his captor anything to go on.

"Now, Footlicker," Dave continued, "you better tell me what happened with -- what was his name? Theron? -- yeah, Theron, or I'm going to have to implement a punishment. You got until five, slave. So let's see here: five ..."

Tom's lips tightened.

"Four ..."

Tom looked away, as if that would somehow prevent this ordeal from even happening.

"Three ..."

Tom remained defiant and silent.

"Oh, I'm going to enjoy this: two ..."

Nothing.

"One ..." said Dave, enthusiasm creeping into his voice.

Tom remained completely motionless.

"Well then!" said Dave, clapping his hands together, "It looks like we got a slaveboy here in a state of total non-compliance. As per the contract he signed with us, this is a big ol' no-no. However, I'm not too worried, dear viewers. And it just so happens that I have some very special friends that are going to help out. Fellas?"

With that, Matt & Red, both with those same black ski-masks drawn over their heads, walked over and sat down on the chairs in front of Tom on either side.

"Now, Footlicker," teased Dave, "would you be so kind as to place your feet into the laps of the gentlemen that sit here before you?"

Realizing what was about to happen, Tom simply remained motionless, in somewhat of a stunned silence all his own.

"Oh, I do love how shy you are, Footlicker," noted Dave, "but you know full well that if we have to grab them ourselves, we will very much do so. Now why don't you be a good little slaveboy and put your feet up so each man here has a foot at their disposal, OK?"

Realizing that Dave was very much speaking the truth, Tom

reluctantly lifted up each pantless leg, and placed one socked foot in Matt's lap, the other in Red's. Both men proceeded to wrap one arm around the leg, keeping it in place, leaving the other hand free to torment those feet so long as they saw fit.

"Gentlemen," started Dave, here in full ringmaster mode, "would you please do the honors of finding out just how utterly ticklish our helpless little Footlicker is?"

The boys didn't need any more encouragement: both men, their fingernails sharp and well-kept, proceeded to drag said nails across the soles of Tom's own socked feet. At first, Tom grimaced, just taken back by the sudden nature of this tickle attack, his body jerking even with his hands still bound behind the chair he was sitting in. His shoulders jerked one way and then another, his legs pumping and fighting as best they could even as the two athletic frat boys kept his legs firmly in place.

"Oh, c'mon Footlicker," Dave said with a devilish glee, "all we want to know is whether your totally straight roommate and friend Theron decided to indulge your totally fuckin' weird obsession with male feet by letting you lick his meaty mantoes. That's all we want to know. And the longer we don't know, the longer we're just gonna keep tickling you ..."

Tom was in pure tickle agony right now, as each master was using their own technique to try and break their owned property. Red was very precise in what he was doing, never overplaying his hand, just using simple, direct drags, pokes, and traces along Tom's instep and arches to try and elicit a response; meanwhile, Matt was going crazy, tapping during one moment, scratching that area where the heel turned into the arch the next, prodding and wiggling as best as he could in-between each toe after that. The sheer lack of consistency between the two tormentors was sending a whole host of mixed signals to Tom's poor brain, and a very reluctant smile started appearing on his face, dragging the corners of his mouth upwards as if by invisible strings that only his tormentors could pull. Fuck, all those tickly sensations on his feet were turning into real laughter spots, and as much as Tom tried curling his toes, he simply couldn't resist any more.

A snicker sneaked out the corner of Tom's mouth, entirely against his will. Then a giggle, and then ... the flood gates fuckin' burst.

"PLEASE!" Tom screamed between full-body chuckles, "Puh-lease!! Stop tickling me!! I -- ha ha fuck godammit -- I can't take much more of this!!"

"Aww, ain't that cute?" noted Dave to the camera, "After writing tome after tone of tickle-fiction, the author himself can't take a measly five minutes of actual foot tickling. Do you like being tickled, Footlicker?"

"NO!" screamed Tom, before returning into laughter so violent he was almost making the chair he was tied to vibrate right along his shuddering body.

"Well," said Dave, drawing out every word just so Tom could *feel* his ticklish punishment last all the longer, "if you don't give me what I want, I guess I'm just going to have to tell the guys to remove your socks in order to continue your punishment ..."

"Theron let me lick his feet!" Tom screamed, which immediately caused Matt & Red to stop their torment. "He really ... he really didn't know what to make of my fetish, but he kind of went all YOLO on me and propped his feet up and ... I got to sniff them ... and lick them ... and suck on his ... his fucking glorious sweet toes." Tom was panting from exhaustion by the end of this.

All the guys in the room seemed to stare at Tom, chest heaving, brow sweating, as he was recounting his tale.

"But," added Dave, "did you get to kiss his feet?"

"What?" shot back Tom, "No! I just ... I just licked and sucked. Then I said I was going to grab something to make this even better and just bolted for it 'cos you said I had to be back within an hour."

"Oh yeah, we did have him do that, didn't we?" noted Red.

"Yeah we did," said Matt, "and the motherfucker was almost late. I was gonna have him make out with my toes until he got a stiffy."

"Do you think he has one now?" asked Red.

"I dunno," started Dave. "Guess there's only one way to find out. J.C., would you mind bringing the scissors over here? No, they should be in a cup next to my keyboard by my computer. Yeah, there you go."

J.C. walked in-frame over to where Tom was sitting, scissors in hand. Red & Matt still had Tom's socked feet clutched in their arms.

"Now sir," Dave said, gesturing to Tom's crotch, "would you do the honors?"

"Um, sure," J.C. said, "I guess."

With that, J.C., notably without a ski-mask of his own, knelt down in front of Tom's crotch and proceeded to carefully take the scissors and start to cut Tom's boxers right off. J.C. was very careful in his handling of this, as he appeared very concerned about making sure not to cut or poke Tom in any way with the scissors, and his diligence paid off, as there wasn't a scratch on him by the time Tom's boxers were in complete tatters, leaving his dick and balls completely exposed for the camera. J.C. began to walk away, but Dave stopped him.

"Hey J.C.," Dave inquired, "would you mind doing me a really devious solid?"

"Um, sure," J.C. said.

"Would you mind standing behind Footlicker, taking off one of your flip-flops and holding it right up to his nose for him to sniff?"

J.C. cocked his eye a little, but was already so far deep that a little bit further didn't appear to be something that would harm anyone. "Um, yeah, sure," he said.

With that, J.C. walked behind the helpless Tom and stepped out of his sandals, picking them up and then holding the toehold area right in the center of Tom's face.

"Now do me a favor, Footlicker," Dave said, "and take a few really big inhales of this motherfucker. Does it smell like feet? Does it smell like desire?"

Tom's head was figiting a bit, but resistance was futile: J.C. must have really worn those sandals just about everywhere, as the smell was absolutely and completely overpowering. Tom really didn't want to admit that he was enjoying it, but one whiff was all it took: it smelled pungent, a bit salty, sweaty, and ... completely fucking desirable. They smelled great. They smelled like everything he ever wanted all in one single place. All those glorious feel-good tingles were making themselves known, and before long ...

"Hey, look! Footlicker is gettin' hard!" shouted Dave, pointing at the slowly-inflating erection on Tom's body. The two guys holding his feet looked back to see if it was in fact real, and it very much was. Tom actually was enjoying the rank smell of J.C.'s footwear before his erection was ridiculed, but now he was flush with embarrassment all over again. "Oh man, this is too great, you guys," Dave said into the camera. "Man, who knows how many internet pervs would pay for this video. We could have a fuckin' cash cow on our hands here."

"And a real footpig to go with it," said Bobby, who was behind the computer desk this whole time.

"What did you say?" asked Dave.

"I said 'and a real footpig to go with it,'" noted Bobby.

"Footpig," said Dave, "I ... I really fuckin' like that. 'Footpig.' Man, that's such a great term. Hey Footlicker: are you a little Footpig?"

Tom remained stoic and silent, trying his best to ... no longer be hard, even as J.C. kept that sandal firmly pressed into his face.

"I said," continued Dave, a mean streak emerging in his voice, "are you a good little footpig? Are you going to oink for me like a footpig?"

Tom tried to not only remain silent, but tried to not breathe through his nostrils so that he wouldn't be turned on by more of J.C.'s footmusk.

"J.C., come back over here," Dave instructed. J.C. threw his sandals back on the floor and stepped in them before walking back behind the camera, the slapping of those flip-flops against his heels as he walked still echoing very much in Tom's mind. "Boys," Dave started, referring to Matt & Red, "would you mind removing Footpig's sock's for him and tickling him until he oinks?"

"With fuckin' pleasure," said Matt through his ski-mask.

That look of panic returned to Tom's face, which made Dave chortle with delight. Tom could feel the two frat guy's hands slowly reach underneath the elastic of his socks and gradually pull them downward, past the ankles, around the soles, and finally off the toes. There Tom was; tied down, naked save his shirt, and now barefoot, legs outstretched in the hands of some truly sadistic motherfuckers. He was scared, no doubt, but ... fuck if this wasn't the stuff some of his letters were made of. The fantasies he always housed of being dominated by these guys tended to be particularly potent, but the reality of the fantasy versus the idealized fun his mind conceived of made for two very, very different experiences. Although parts of what was going on were registering as "hot" in his mind, deep down, Tom remained completely and totally scared by what was going to happen next.

"Make him squeal, boys," Dave ordered -- and the boys needed no further encouragement.

Tom actually yelped as his captors started tickling his feet, the laughter sometimes cutting him off mid-breath, making for a heady rush in almost no time at all. Red continued his very exact, very precise fingering of his soles, while Matt continued his wildman approach, diving into Tom's foot with total abandon. Tom arched his back, twisted as best as he could in his chair, guffawed and laughed and attempted to plea through shortened laugh-stained breaths. It was overwhelming. He was a giggle machine, and those boys had the controls.

After about two minutes of relentless foot scrapings lighting his brain on fire with smiles, the corners of Tom's mouth were hurting from being forced into such a brutal twisted smile as the one he had now. The scratches just kept on tickling and tickling and tickling, Dave occasionally trying to egg Tom on, saying "C'mon, Footpig: oink for me! Oink like the footpig you are!" Tom's brain was near its breaking point, the word "TICKLE" flashing in his skull in gigantic marquee letters. He couldn't resist anymore, his mouth unable to shut from the flood of laughter that was just spewing out of it, and then, finally, he broke:

"OINK OINK OINK!" he shouted between stifled laughter. "I'M YOUR FOOTPIG! OINK OINK OINK!"

Dave and the other guys all began laughing at the same time: they thought this was just nothing short of amusing. "Oh man!" Dave exclaimed, "He did it! He actually fucking did it! Oh, well done, footpig! Guys, give him a breather."

Matt & Red ceased their relentless torture of Tom's feet, even letting them go from their arms so they could simply retract close to Tom's body, bending for the first time in a long time after being held and stretched out for such devious tickle torture. Tom, still naked except for his shirt, couldn't do much of anything aside from taking in deep, deep breaths, slowly regaining his centered self. Matt & Red's hooded faces has turned in their chairs just to look at their weakened slaveboy try and regain his composure.

"How was that, little footpig?" asked Dave, coyly.

"It was," Tom panted, "it was fucking brutal, sir."

"Awww," Dave purred, "I do love me an honest footpig -- don't you guys?" The rest of the room gave a general sound of agreement.

"Now Footpig," Dave continued, "do you want to go through another brutal round of tickle torture?"

"No sir!" Tom said, violently shaking his head.

"Do you want us to let you go so you can just pass out and regain all the energy we so mercilessly sucked out of you?"

"Yes," Tom said, still panting.

"OK, then you have to answer us one question. Just one question. Can you do that for us, Footpig?"

"Yes," Tom said, still taking in a few bucket breaths now and then, "I can do that."

"Tell me, Footpig," Dave said, "of all the guys here, whose feet are you *most* attracted to?"

Tom didn't even give it a second thought "Bobby's."

"Whoa!" Dave exclaimed. "I did *not* see that one coming! Bobby, have you been teasing this pathetic little footpig with your toes?"

"I don't think I've even taken off my socks around him," Bobby noted off-camera.

"Wow, that's amazing," Dave noted, "hadn't even seen his goddamn toes and is still crazy about 'em. Man, have you guys ever heard anything so pathetic?"

"Let me go and put all my socks away then," Bobby said, making his way out of Dave's room.

"He's got a good point there," Dave noted to Tom, "Bobby is, after all, doing us a favor of housing you and your foot-obsessed mind, so it's only natural that he would feel the need to put a couple of safeguards in place if not just to prevent you from going crazy when he's not there. Don't you think that's wise of him, footpig?"

"Yes sir," Tom said, simply leaving his head sagging and looking at the floor, so as not to have direct eye contact with any of his tormentors.

"Awww, Footpig is tired, ain't he?" Dave asked.

"Yes sir," Tom repeated.

"Matt, why don't you let him out so that he can crawl back to his quarters and think about how much he enjoyed doing what he did."

"OK," said Matt, walking behind the chair Tom was bound to with scissors in hand, "but I think we should let him crawl out of here only after he's properly kissed our fuckin' toes."

"Ooh, that's a great idea," noted Dave. "J.C.: why don't you unscrew the camera so we can have a nice handheld moment here. Gentlemen: why don't you all slip off yer shoes so that Footpig here has something to truly, honestly be grateful for. Footpig, you get on the ground -- where you fuckin' belong."

Matt's final snip of the zip-toes was done, and Tom's arms naturally went back in front of him, each hand taking turns to caress his wrists, as the imprints from the zip-ties was very prominent.

"I said *on the floor,* Footpig!" Dave shouted.

Without hesitating, Tom just learned forward and collapsed face-down on the floor in front of him. He looked around and saw the boys untying their shoelaces, slipping off sneakers, or hastily removing their socks. Tom could see J.C.'s flip-flopped toes walking over towards him, and looked up to see the big expensive camera was now on a shoulder-mount.

"Now go on," commanded Matt, who was now completely unshod, "kiss my toes and tell me they're wonderful."

Tom looked at lightly tan toes before him and couldn't help but be intrigued: those toes were perfectly shaped, the toenails reflecting that perfect amount of dulled shine, everything looking delicious and delightful. Tom didn't need any extraneous forces to convince him, he arched his head up, leaned in, and planted a light kiss on the tops of Matt's toes on his right foot.

"Yeah, keep kissing 'em, bitch," Matt ordered, clearly relishing such a flagrant act of out-and-out submission. Tom leaned in and kept kissing and kissing and kissing: the index toe, the top of the foot, one of the big toes, over and over again."

"OK, now mine," asserted Red, and Tom swiveled on the ground to see the dom's mighty toe meat before him, thick and brutish and all sorts of pale wonderful. Tom again started kissing those meat monsters and couldn't help but feel turned on by doing it. After all, here he was submitting to the natural power and beauty that was male toes, the most divine and incredible force ever to be seen in this universe. Kissing them only made his deep-seated connection to them all the stronger, and as exhausted as he was from the torment that was just inflicted upon him, each toe-kiss brought Tom a sort of quiet erotic strength all his own, and once he started, he simply couldn't bring himself to stop.

"Alright," Dave said after a couple of minutes, "you've had enough with the other boys, now it's my turn."

Amazingly, this was actually the first time Tom got to see Dave's naked toes -- and they weren't bad. Very standard-issue: no hairs on the tops or on the toes, pretty pale, very soft (which Tom determined was from the fact that Dave wasn't much of a barefooter in any way, shape, or form), but they still carried a charm all their own.

For whatever reason, Tom took a quieter approach in handling Dave's own digits, making very light, soft, gentle kisses, almost romantic in nature. Even to Tom's lips, the skin felt softer than the other guys'. They radiated a much quieter masculinity, but Tom was no less intrigued. Dave, being Dave, of course noticed the change in kissing tone.

"Oh man, you're being so delicate with my tootsies, ain't ya?" Dave laughed. "Maybe we'll end up calling this movie *Romancing the Toe*. I think there might be some people that get it just for the title alone."

Tom remained quiet as he softly peppered the tops of Dave's feet with kisses. His eyes kept glancing over, however, to the untamed sandal-clad toes of J.C. Dave noticed as well.

"Oh buddy!" he shouted, "I think the Footpig just found a new truffle to snarf on. Oh, I like that twist. Yeah, go over and kiss the camera man's toes, Footpig. Make him glad he came."

Tom scooted over a bit without questioning his new directive, and got a nice close glimpse of the toes and sandals that he had to sniff on camera earlier. Tom was so far deep in this that any sense of dignity had long since been abolished. While he's down here, on camera, he might as well enjoy it, and began deeply, passionately kissing J.C.'s toes. The first kiss kind of freaked the cameraman out, almost causing him to step back, but J.C. soon adjusted to the bizarre-yet-pleasing sensation. These kisses were wet, sloppy, and some of that saliva began seeping down in-between his toes. Tom somewhat caught this himself, but also didn't really care that much: J.C.'s toes were just too fucking fun to kiss.

"Dude," Dave exclaimed, "he's going to town on your digits, brah! Why don't you go ahead and just fuckin' make out with those toes, Footpig?"

It appeared J.C. was about to say something, but Tom wasn't even going to let him start: he immediately took his tongue and began slurping at J.C.'s toes, licking along the base all the way to the tips, extracting as much flavor as he could from the spaces in-between, unable or unwilling to stop this meeting of mouth and toe unlike anyone had ever seen. J.C.'s camera pointed downward and captured as much as it could.

Tom began licking the tops of J.C.'s feet in big, broad licks, at which point J.C. actually took two steps away from Tom mid-lick.

"Dude, that fuckin' tickles," J.C. said, still filming even as he did so.

"Alright," Dave said, "I think he's had enough. Shut the camera off." J.C. took the big unwieldy device down from his shoulders, apparently relieved now that he wasn't luggin' the big thing.

"OK, Footpig," Dave continued, "you can go back to your room, but you have to crawl there the entire way, OK?"

"OK," Tom agreed.

"Now get out of my sight," the barefoot Dave commanded, and Tom needed no further motivation. On all fours, he slowly crawled out of the room, leaving his bevy of tormentors behind, but, strangely, feeling very positive about the experience, especially getting the chance to suck on the dirty hippie filmmaker toes of J.C. That proved to be a treat in and of itself -- worth losing most of his clothes over.

As Tom worked his way out the hallway on all fours, he was able to successfully maneuver his way down the stairs without any incident. By the time he got to the main landing, he noticed there were some other brothers moving around the house, some of them barefoot themselves. One was very tall, muscular, and bearded ... and the dude barely even acknowledged the crawling, mostly-naked footpig before him. Despite his big, shapely, hairy athlete feet, he walked on by the boy without any regard. Strange, thought Tom, as the only way that could happen is if his tormentors had warned the rest of the frat what was going on with their newest resident. Then again, Tom shouldn't be too surprised: all the guys in collusion together made up half the frat, it seemed. Of course, everything would go the way Red says it will. Maybe the tall athlete guy's dismissal wasn't too surprising after all.

By the time he made it back to Bobby's room, the door was open, and he crawled his way in. Bobby briefly glanced at him, but otherwise remained staring at his computer, headphones glued to his ears just as before. Tom crawled past him, past that damn black wire media stand, and onto his oval of space cleared out near the windows. A bit tired from all the crawling, Tom pulled out a new pair of boxers from his duffel bag, put them on, then just rolled over onto his side, again making a make-shift pillow of out of some clothes he brought with him.

"Thank you," Tom said, exhaustively, towards Bobby. The bearded one took of his headphones to address Tom.

"What now?"

"Thank you," Tom said, "for leaving the room and not participating the way you did. Like ... really. Thank you."

"Strange," Bobby shot back, "from what you said, sounds like you would've actually liked to taste *my* toes most of all."

"I mean," stammered Tom a bit, "yeah, but, I mean ... you're not ... you don't appear to be mean. The other guys just seem to be, ya know, really enjoying having me as their footpig ..."

"God," Bobby moaned, "you're already using their terminology."

"No," Tom backpedaled, "it's just ... you're not like the rest of them and, ya know, you don't have to do anything for me or anything 'cos I know you're doing enough but, ya know, just ... thank you."

Bobby cocked his eyebrow a bit and stared back at the boy who was occupying the same room as him. It seemed like Bobby kind of almost wanted to say something out of turn, but then resigned himself to an old trope:

"Just ... just don't sniff my socks, OK?"

"You got it, boss," said Tom, strangely gleeful with his response.

Bobby smirked a bit but then just put back on his headphones and started at his computer screen.

Tom, meanwhile, was too exhausted to even think about anything. He was so tired, his brain could barely even comprehend what he had actually just been through. It didn't even feel real: it was more just a series of images that played out in his mind, but Tom felt strangely disconnected from them.

No matter though: within seconds, that exhaustion was going to knock him out. Tom went to plug his phone into the wall charger near where his head rested, and shortly thereafter, just dozed off into a deep, heavy sleep.

CHAPTER SIX: The Deal

Bobby's alarm once again started up, slowly arousing Tom from his tired, heavy sleep. He had no dreams, but simply a series of thoughts that flew through his head at night, images and distinct memories (and smells) from the night before. Tom's mind was having a hard time dividing the line between what he wanted and what he didn't, as this mixture of actual foot worship, aggro heterosexual dominance, and untold amounts of humiliation was proving to be a bit much to wrap his head around. He loved some of it but regretted other parts even worse. It seemed like every hour of his life now was equal parts pure heaven and undeniable hell. The fact that there was such an overt sexual component seemed to be the glue that was keeping this together, much less going forward with this whole ordeal.

"Hey Tom," Bobby said weakly, his arm flopping out of his bedsheets vainly trying to hit his snooze alarm.

"Yes?" asked Tom, groggy himself.

"Can you," Bobby exhaustedly sputtered, "can you hit that for me?"

"Sure," Tom said, crawling on all fours up to the head of Bobby's bed, tapping the oversized Snooze button on the alarm, Bobby's head soon burying itself in its pillow again. Tom could hear a very muffled "thanks" come from the boy, but soon drifted off into his own kingdom of dreams. Tom carefully crawled back to his sleeping area, but he knew his own body quite well: by being even a bit awakened like this, he knew full well that getting back to sleep was a tall order. Guessing he was probably up before anyone else, Tom unzipped his duffel bag, pulled out a towel that he forgot he packed, and proceeded to make his way to the Frat house shower. Just as he suspected, no one was there, and Tom got to try and scrub as much of the sweat and shame that had dried on him from the night before. He got dressed, put his stuff back in the room (tip-toeing carefully so as not to awake Bobby from his slumber), and grabbed his phone, laptop, and messenger bag and then made his way to the cafeteria again, getting ready for another day of class.

The routine was roughly the same: filling his mouth with cereal as his he scrolled tried to complete another online quiz, his email still popped open on a separate window. There a few class updates, and, of course, Theron's message, still there, still unanswered. The guilt over that weighed heavily on Tom's head, but at this point, it would almost feel worse to him trying to explain all this to Theron, despite the fact that it was obviously the "right" thing to do. Tom sighed a bit at the thought. He had absolutely no idea how the rest of this was going to work out, as there was no "conclusion" his mind could think of, no light at the end of the tunnel. Did he really want a light though? Did he really want to escape? Or was his Hell also doubling over as a private kind of horny Heaven?

Tom's phone buzzed. He had a new text message. Tom slid open the lock screen, and it was a message from a number he didn't recognize. It was a picture message, and ... holy fuck.

Staring right at Tom's eyeballs was a picture of the tops of Matt's toes. Tom immediately recognized them, the shape of those lightly tanned beauties already burned into the back of his brain. They were shaply, slender, beautiful, all the way down to the way that Matt had kept the shape of his toenails in: nicely treated but not to the point of obsessive manicure. They were just ... transfixing. They were long enough to warrant a knuckle, and Tom was assuredly not opposed to admiring every single aspect of such masculine, powerful, and downright sexy feet.

Another message followed. This one a text from Matt. "You like that, bitch?"

Tom gulped upon seeing that. I mean, Matt was correct, he did, but with such an aggressive tone, Tom wondered what would happen by responding in the affirmative. Then again, he also realized that he didn't have much of a choice in the matter either.

"Yes sir," he started typing back, "I think they are very handsome and sexy." Send.

Another response seconds later: "That's what I thought. You want to lick them, right? Suck the flavor out of 'em while you work your little footpig boner?"

Tom gulped again. Damn he was good.

"Of course, sir," he typed back. Send.

One more response: "Well then you're going to score me some green. Eight of an ounce would be fab. We're gonna need it for tonight. Make it happen or I'm sending your hard drive contents to every single fucking person you know."

Tom held his phone, staring at the message, his fingers trembling slightly. Tom had been around people who have smoked weed before, and assuredly didn't mind it (although he didn't partake himself -- it was important for him to keep his mind sharp for his studies at all times), but ... scoring weed? Buying some? First off, Tom had absolutely zero dollars to his name right now (well a few in his account, but barely enough for a meal, much less a bag of weed). Secondly, he had absolutely no idea who among his friends would even know how to get weed. What if one of his straight-laced buddies actually was some sort of narc? What would he have to do then?

Suddenly, worry stretched across his forehead, filling up his entire frontal lobe. As Tom noted the time and how he should really get a move on to his first class, he frantically began looking at every single student as a potential mark. As he crossed the campus in the crisp morning air, every face was registering as a candidate. Goth girl Vicki? Maybe. The EDM-loving Brian? Perhaps. The rat-faced odd duck who just went by the name Ling? It was like Tom's own head began filling up with a paranoia all its own.

As classes progressed, again, whatever the teachers were talking about registered as some sort of mute dumbshow, their gestures and writings on the board coming off as completely illegible to Tom, as his mind couldn't intake any new information right now in his frantic state. Instead, his eyes darted around his classrooms, period-to-period, looking for those who were maybe a bit antagonistic, those who were a bit anti-authority, maybe even those specific types of loners that were just looking for some sort of escape to their problems. Tom's eyes were drawn to any guy who had those weird kind of black studs in their earlobes, but never once did Tom feel the strength inside to try and approach them. Even in his Intro to Acting class, which took place actually on the stage where all the campus' theatre productions went up, had a Southern-bred boy named Johnny who loved dancing, grown-up Miley Cyrus, and often told casual stories of his weed use. Even during class when he went barefoot and acting as country as a chicken coop, Tom still just couldn't get past how strange and bizarre it was to try and ask one of his friends for weed. Plus, how does one go about it? Does one simply say "Hey, you got any weed to sell?" Do you send an email about it? Tom just had never learned and wasn't ever in a position to figure it out.

The big campus-wide bell rang. Class was over, lunch time right up around the corner. Tom put his messenger bag around his shoulder and made his way out the theatre. Right as he was exiting the campus' Fine Arts building to make his way over to the cafeteria, he passed the stairway that lead out the building, but saw a guy from one of his classes, Christopher, having a phone conversation next to the stairs that lead to the classrooms on the second floor.

"Naw man," he said, "It's $80 for an eighth. This isn't anything new. Yeah, well, hey, you let me know if you have it by tonight otherwise I ain't swingin' by. Got it? Jeez."

Christopher ended the call a bit frustrated. Christopher was a nice guy, judging by the limited interactions Tom had had with him. A bit rotund, Christopher nonetheless carried himself well: his scruffy beard was nicely shaped and the product of a lot of effort. He often wore a baseball cap, and had a new pair of sneakers that he wore every single day. He considered himself a bit of a sneakerhead, buying up one-offs and strange brands on a semi-frequent basis. Tom had overheard some excitable conversations that he had before wherein he talked about getting in a new pair, adding it to his self-described collection of "shoeporn." He was kind of attractive in a rugged sort of way, but moreover, he was a guy that was often bristling with optimism, a very upbeat person to talk to.

"Everything OK?" Tom asked, approaching him in a very uncharacteristic fashion, given the two hadn't had many one-on-one conversations before.

"Oh, yeah," Chris said, a bit surprised to be approached by the somewhat nerdy Tom, "I'm just, ya know, dealing with people who don't realize that goods and services can't be paid with perpetual I.O.U.'s, ya know?"

"They want the weed, they just don't want to *pay* for it, right?" noted Tom, boldly asserting that that's what they were talking about.

"Ha, yeah," said Christopher, smiling, "people can be real assholes, sometimes."

"Do you *only* accept cash as payment?" asked Tom. Christopher arched his eyebrow a bit.

"I mean," he started, "generally, yeah. That's how it works. Usually, anyways."

"What if someone owed you a favor?" asked Tom, a bit in disbelief by the very words that were coming out if his mouth.

"Um," stammered Christopher, "what *kind* of favor?"

Tom's mind raced, and the ideas that were suddenly popping up in his head didn't even seem to be like his own.

"You got a class right now?" asked Tom.

"Nope, just lunch. Why?"

Tom's eyes darted around a bit. "Here, follow me upstairs."

"Um ... I mean ... OK." Christopher was game, perhaps surprising Christopher the most. The boys went up the stairs to see the big ol' hall of classrooms that made up the Fine Arts building. Even with the lunch period being active for some, the boys looked and saw that while some classes were still going, they eventually found that the choir room was completely empty.

"In here," noted Tom.

The room was a very unremarkable shade of gray, the chairs on different levels all facing the podium in the middle, the blackboard behind it permanently etched with lines for music notes to be drawn over them. Tom gestured to Christopher to sit down in a chair right in the middle of the classroom. This being a liberal arts college, the door leading to the hallway didn't lock, but Tom had no other choice but to take his chance here.

"Um, what's going on?" asked the sitting Christopher, setting his backpack down by the chair, a bit confused by what's happening.

"Well," started Tom, "I ... I really need an eighth, and I do no have the financial means to assist in that transaction -- but I think you're a good guy, and I don't ever want to leave you with an I.O.U., so ya know, I figure you could use a little something different."

"Whoa dude," Christopher started, "I mean, I'm flattered and all, but, ya know, I'm not gay. I mean, really, if it was any other context, I could accept a blowjob, but as it stands right now, I just ..."

"No no no," interjected Tom, "I'm sorry, I ... wasn't going to blow you."

"Oh," noted Christopher, a bit surprised, "then what were you going to do then?"

"Can you trust me for just a half-second here?" asked Tom.

"Um, yeah, I guess," said Christopher.

Tom sported a wry grin at the response. He bent over and began unlacing Christopher's shoes, the shoelaces a bright designer red.

"Hey hey hey," Christopher started, "you gotta be careful with that.

These are limited edition."

"Oh I know," said Tom, somewhat seductively, "but to be brutally honest, I don't really care much about them. All I really care about is what's *inside* them."

Fully unlaced, Tom slipped off the big cushy sneaker that Christopher was wearing. There was a thick white ankle-sock underneath, the bottoms that classic murky gray look from lots of overuse. Tom, unable to help himself, placed his nostril just underneath Christopher's big socked toe and took in a big ol' sniff. Tom's lungs expanded, filling his entire body with true erotic delight. Christopher, meanwhile, had absolutely no idea what was transpiring.

"What ... the literal fuck is happening, man?" Christopher asked.

"Trust me," Tom coyly shot back, unlacing the other shoe as he spoke, "this will be worth it in the end."

With that, Tom wound up slipping of Christopher's other shoe, leaving the burly man sitting sock-footed in the middle of an empty college choir room. Tom's hand was near Christopher's left socked foot, and he could feel the warmth absolutely radiate out of it.

"So," Christopher started, "I gather you're really getting off of on this, right? You like socks?"

"Oh no," Tom said, hooking his fingers underneath the elastic loops of the tops of Christopher's socks, "I got a fetish for *feet*. Guys' feet especially. Don't ask me why, but I think they are just the fuckin' sexiest thing in the world." At this point, Christopher's left sock was off, and Tom got a glimpse of Christopher's beautiful toes: a bit stubby, but very manly, the toes being broader and thicker than any of the ones he's had to worship since this entire ordeal started. It was a true feast for the senses. Tom then proceeded to remove Christopher's other sock.

"Um, dude," Christopher started, "I don't think this is going to--"

"Close your eyes, dude," Tom ordered, "I just want you to focus on the sensation right now, and just let it totally wash over you, OK?"

"Um," started Christopher.

"Shut 'em," Tom said.

Christopher did so. Tom then picked up Christopher's right foot, sticking so beautifully out of his blue jeans, and slowly, carefully, wrapped his lips around Christopher's big toe. He started off sucking very quietly, very subtly, and very, very sensuously. He slowly moved to the left, individually taking in each toe in descending order, sucking the flavor of it so succinctly, so powerfully, coating each one with his saliva as the tips of his teeth lightly scraped the tops and bottoms of each piece of toemeat. In truth, Tom was lost in the moment, even as there was a part of his brain that knew that he had no idea what Christopher was thinking of this whole ordeal. So far, Christopher wasn't making any sounds nor was he pulling his feet away, but that in and of itself was more than enough for Tom to keep going.

He soon stopped and picked up Christopher's left foot, this time not focusing on the sucking of toes so much as he was the heel, lifting Christopher's foot above his head, then dropping the heel into his mouth, his lips wrapping around as much of that curved right angle as he could, before dragging his suction hole right above the heel, soon bringing out the tongue for proper slurpings of Christopher's wide, beefy soles.

As Tom licked and licked his little footpig heart out, he shot a glance on over to Christopher's face, and noted that the man himself was still keeping his eyes shut, his lips slightly pursed, no doubt using the sensation that was running through him as a means to plumb some well-known erotic depths he had inside of him. Realizing this, Tom stopped licking for a moment, and simply waited.

After about 20 seconds, Christopher opened his eyes to see Tom staring right at him. "What, that was it?" he asked.

"I mean, do you *want* me to keep going?" Tom asked.

"Yeah, man," Christopher said, closing his eyes again. "It's really fuckin' weird but I won't lie: it feels pretty fuckin' good ..."

"Then allow me," continued Tom. He tried to put as many of the toes on Christopher's left foot in his mouth as he could, just soaking his own mouth in all the foot flavor it could possibly handle, his throat coated with the stuff. Each toe was being given special toe-sucking treatment, but Tom made sure to also snake his agile tongue in-between each toe, really lubricating that tender place that exists between them. Each time he did so, he noted that Christopher sported a bit of a grin, no doubt meaning that he was getting to him somehow.

As he sucked that big toe more and more though, he noticed that Christopher's left hand was down to his crotch, squeezing that package inside his jeans just a bit. If this was a casual thing Tom spotted in class, he wouldn't necessarily think he was massaging his own hardon, but given that it was just the two of them right now, and Tom's mouth was currently acting as Christopher's sock, the intent was obvious.

"Whip it out," Tom instructed when not smothering his tongue 'tween Christopher's toes. "Whip it out and work it."

Christopher needed no further encouragement. Undoing his belt and unzipping his jeans with great speed, Christopher pulled his uncut, very wide dick from his boxers, and it appeared to have been hard for some time now. It was horny enough that the top of his foreskin could no longer keep up with the expansion of his horniness, his deep pink cockhead visible through the top of the skin. Christopher's own hand reached down and began pumping away, which was as big a cue as any for Tom to really go down on this somewhat-skater boy's soles.

Tom licked with a fury, doing his best to evenly distribute his deep slurpings so that there was no part of Christopher's bare feet that was dry. He slurped, sucked, licked, and then slurped, sucked, and licked some more. The speed of Christopher's pumpings was increasing slightly. Tom egged him on with short phrases when he could: "That's it." "Keep it going." "Work it."

Finally, after starting a really big, long, slow drag of Christopher's left sole, from heel to toe-base, Christopher let out a brief, high-pitched moan. The pitch was going up as he was getting closer, closer, closer to ... fuckin' incredible climax. Christopher shot a solid load all over the dark hoodie he was wearing, followed by another one that was almost as intense, and then another one of lesser power, then another, then another. Tom stopped licking the naked feet of this masculine man, and just stared at Christopher's face, his mouth forming that look of someone coming down from pure ecstasy, the eyes still remaining closed the entire time.

Slowly, surely, Christopher came back to reality, opening his eyes, seeing the doe-eyed looking Tom just staring at him from where his naked foot was.

"Well, um," started Christopher, obviously a bit shaken by the sheer circumstance of events he just experienced, "can you maybe see if there are some paper towels or something around?"

"Oh sure, no problem," said Tom, getting to his feet and looking around. As he did this, Christopher slipped his wet feet into his socks and shoes.

"Oh hey," Tom said, "I'm not finding anything anything."

"It's OK," Christopher said, tying up his laces, "I'll just stuff my hoodie in my backpack. No one will be the wiser."

Christopher took off his hoodie and rolled it into a ball as best as he could. He zipped open his backpack but kind of stared for a second, then took his gaze over to Tom.

"So, you did all of that for an eighth?"

"Yeah," said Tom, "I mean, if I had the money, I'd give it to you, but I also wanted to show you that I was very serious about repayment."

"Well," Christopher started in a drawn out way, "I mean ... I haven't ... done ... anything ... quite like that."

"Few have," Tom retorted.

"Heh, you're probably right," Christopher agreed. "Here, have this."

Out of his backpack, Christopher pulled out a small plastic container, the kind that sandwiches are usually kept in.

"I think you've earned this."

Tom looked inside and could see, in a nice thin plastic bag, was a good hefty amount of weed. An eighth, he gathered.

"Well, thanks man," Tom said. "Let me know if you ever have any other denominations like this you need to get rid of."

"Tom," Christopher said, slinging his backpack over his shoulder as he readied to leave, "I'll *always* have stuff to get rid of." Christopher buttoned that sentence with a quick little wink.

With that, Christopher left the room, leaving Tom with his tongue tasting of man feet and a small container full of weed in his hand. He couldn't have scripted this better if he had to. A pleased smile stretched across his face. He couldn't believe his luck. If this is what the fates had in store for him, this was going to be nothing short of an amazing day.

CHAPTER SEVEN: The Rooster

"I have your stuff," Tom texted to Matt, providing no more details than what was needed. Tom was walking across the campus to his final class, a sense of accomplishment filling up his bones.

"Wut, rly?" Matt texted back. Tom was unsure how to respond to that but received another response just as quickly: "Sweet man. Looks like you'll get to meet The Rooster 2nite."

Tom jerked his head back a bit upon reading that. The Rooster? What the fuck was Matt even talking about?

Then, of course, the obvious response hit Tom: Matt was referring to his penis. While there's nothing inherently wrong with that, Tom was honestly a bit frightened by the notion. With his male foot fetish having developed so strongly in his teens, everything toeward became his automatic focus and obsession: he hadn't had a lot of time to really dive in to the arts of full-blown cocksucking, much less fucking. He still *enjoyed* cock, make no mistake (aesthetically, it was an incredibly beautiful thing to look at), but there were those lingering doubts in his mind: STDs, HIV, every possible bad thing that could happen from just casually ingesting the seed of another man. Tom was always the kind of person who, even if he tossed his clothes on the floor of his room when he got back from classes each day, still was worried about more specifically-hygenic things. Thus, he was worried about Matt's proposition. Admittedly, despite his reservations, he was still fundamentally *curious* to try it, but perhaps not in a scenario such as this.

As the day wore on, this whole cock thing was the only thing he could possibly think about. He wound up grabbing an early dinner from the cafeteria as per usual, but upon seeing Theron enter the cafeteria just as he filled up his plate, he tried to wolf down as much as he could before bolting. The last thing he wanted was to have to have another encounter with his roommate. He exited without making any sort of eye contact (as far as he could tell), and made his way back to the Frat, going straight to Bobby's room without incident.

Bobby was gone, which was fine by Tom's count. He got to his sleeping area and plugged in his laptop, going through as much schoolwork as he could before that dreaded 6pm rolled around, officially making him Matt's property for the rest of the night. For whatever reason, having that looming timed deadline over his head was actually making Tom concentrate on his work easier, perhaps because he knew that if he got too distracted, 6pm would crawl up on him and he would 100% be unable to finish any other work (he could only imagine how poor a negotiation with these frat boys would actually turn out). Once one paper was written, he'd go on to the next quiz, and once that was done, he'd do some research for another class -- man, if only he knew the unyielding power of a deadline before. He could've been so much more productive.

Tom finished his last feasible assignment that he could do: another goddamn online quiz, but hey, it worked out just fine. Tom checked his computer clock: 5:46pm. Hmm, he had some spare time for once. What to do: micro-nap? Facebook time-wasting? He was strangely unmotivated to do either, and tilted his head away from the screen a bit: he'd been staring at it for far too long. Then, he spotted something in the room: next to the foot of Bobby's bed, there appeared to actually be ... a pair of Bobby's used socks. He could see where the base of the toes would be, and they were a deep gray, a sign of having been worn quite excessively or during a time of great sweating and ... Tom was very intrigued.

He knew the big rule that Bobby gave him: not to sniff his socks, but, hey, his room was already unkempt, and Bobby hadn't been home all day, so, hey, why not take a risk? Tom memorized the position where it was at, felt he could properly put them back without raising any suspicion, and ... well fuck it: he grabbed those fuckers up and placed them immediately next to his nose, soon inhaling as much as he could of it.

Holy fuck.

The scent immediately went up his nostrils and straight into his skull, filling up the entirety of his cranium, smothering his brain in this pungent, powerful, incredible scent. It was the smell of sweat, the smell of masculinity, the smell of a boy who had just worked too hard on any given day. It was delicious. It was immediate. It was unlike anything he had smelled before and yet so similar to all of the foot fetish totems he's collected throughout the years. This was his everything.

Tom took in another deep scent, and it only seemed to enhance what was already there. There was a tingly part at the top of his brain, like some sort of pleasure center had just been flipped on by the great taste, scent, and boy oh lord was it making him all sorts of happy. That rush -- both of the actual scent of someone he liked, plus the fact that it was enmeshed with the notion of doing something very naughty -- was intoxicating. Tom had just stumbled across what was a treasure chest full of footpleasure, and right now his brain, his body, and his stiffening dick were all enjoying it. Tom could masturbate *just* to the scent of Bobby's socks if he wanted to, but thought better of it -- the last thing he wanted to do right now was underperform for Matt, who would no doubt be able to tell whether or not Tom had gotten off beforehand.

Carefully, Tom set Bobby's socks back to where they once were. He glanced at the clock again: 5:57pm. He texted Matt: "Hey, so am I just meeting you up in your room?" Tom set his phone down and unzipped his backpack, revealing the small plastic container full of weed that he managed to score earlier, still a bit in disbelief over how it all went down. He popped open one of the lid's corners and took a small sniff of the wrapped buds inside, and was a bit overwhelmed by that green stank of a smell. Really, this is what people get into? They smoke this stuff? Seemed really weird ...

The text alert on his phone just went off. Of course, it was from Matt: "get the fuck up here noww"

Tom needed no further encouragement.

He figured this was a frat house, so there was no need to disclose his little weed container, so proceeded to exit Bobby's room with it in hand and nothing else on his person. He made it around to the staircase, passing a few guys along the way whom he still hadn't been properly introduced to. They no doubt knew about the foot-obsessed capture that was mingling their hardwoods, but none of 'em seemed to give him any mind. Most of 'em were walking around in nicely-worn tan Rainbow flip-flops. Tom couldn't help but catch his own eyes darting to such divine specimens, but knew there was a greater task at hand, and worked his way up to Matt's room.

There it was: with a big dark-brown, generic door in front of it. He rapped on the door twice, and then heard Matt say "Get the fuck in here, footpig!" Tom didn't need to be told twice.

Matt's room was surprisingly small: there was a small twin bed that seemed to basically take up about half the space, with one closet in the wall, one cabinet for clothes, and then just a whole mess of things tossed about on the floor: clothes, computer chargers, DVD cases that were mostly cracked open, the usual bachelor ephemera. Matt was laying on his side in a gray tanktop, ratty blue jeans, and, strangely, some bright yellow socks. His voice was still full of bulldog bite, though, even when in full recline.

"Shut the fucking door!" he ordered. Tom closed it behind him, all his the sheer volume of Matt's voice started making him feel all sorts of nervous.

"Now," Matt continued, a bit more calmly, "why don't you show me the good work that you did today?"

Tom tossed Matt the small little container with the weed. Matt opened it up, pulled out the small bag inside wrapped up with weed, and took a big deep inhale, almost as deep as when Tom sniffed Bobby's discarded socks. Matt's socked toes curled a bit as his lungs expanded: boy was really enjoying what was being fed to his senses.

"Oh, man!" he exclaimed, "This is some top-notch shit right here. I'm kind of amazed you actually were able to score some -- you don't strike me as the tokin' type."

"No," Tom said sheepishly, "I guess not."

"Well tell me," Matt said, a curious purr in his voice, "what did you have to *do* in order to get this weed?"

"Um," Tom started, a bit nervous, "I just had to do some things that I wasn't ... expecting."

"Heh, did they involve *feet*?" Matt intoned.

"Um, yeah," Matt said, trailing off hoping that Matt would just drop it.

"Well, here's another question for you footlicker: have you ever been *high* before?"

"I ... I can't say that I have, no."

Matt then proceeded to reach over to his closet (which, given how small the room was, he could do so without moving too much), and pulled out a big glass bong. It had a light shade of green to it, but was more sleek than it was covered in unnecessary decorations. There was already some water swishing around in the lower chamber, and it looked clean, as if Matt had already taken a great deal of time to prep it for tonight's encounter. Matt unwrapped the weed from the cheap clear sandwich bag it was rapped in, and began packing it into the bowl in the bong's chamber.

"You know, that really does surprise me," Matt started, "I figured you nerdy types always needed a good way to unwind, or maybe just cause your brain to go dumb while you explore the wonders of whatever RPG game you're playing at the time or whatever. Then again, I'm surprised by how many people don't do weed, almost as often as I'm surprised by the people that actually *do*." As he spoke, he was lightly tearing and packing in those flakes of green goodness like someone who had done this hundreds of times before. "Thus, while some people's first-time experiences result in them not even getting high, largely due to the fact that the brain doesn't know what's happening to it, I'm not going to allow that to happen to you, no. Instead, I'm going to overwhelm you with weed, and you are going to be transported to another realm. The realm where ... The Rooster reigns over all."

Matt appeared to be about done packing his bowl to the brim with weed when Tom timidly asked his question: "So, um, who is the Rooster?"

"Hah!" Matt chortled. "'Who is the Rooster?' That's classic. I'll be honest: the Rooster doesn't come out very much, and it's been driving me fuckin' loco, but man, once you smoke this, everything's gonna make a lot more sense ..."

He handed Tom the glass bong. Tom grabbed the lengthy pipe but appeared unsure of how to manipulate it. Matt chuckled a bit. "OK, so you put the base in-between your legs there. Got it? OK, now put your mouth over the cylinder at the top. Good? Now, when you light that little bowl of weed there, you're going to inhale, and the smoke will hit the bong water. Once there is enough in there, you'll keep inhaling as you remove the bowl, and all that beautiful smoke will shotgun down your lungs. Keep it there, hold it there. You'll probably cough, but the longer you hold it, the more ... elevated you will be. Got it?"

"Um, got it," said Tom, slightly unsure of what was about to happen next.

"Now get to it while I get ready," Matt ordered, who went to the corner of his room and appeared to be changing into something. Given there was only a small orange lamp illuminating the wood-paneled room, Matt's shadowed figure could very well have been doing anything. Tom did what he could not to pay attention though, and did as Matt commanded by lighting up the bowl of sticky weed while putting his mouth over the cylinder.

As he lit and inhaled, a billowing cloud of white weedsmoke filled up the base and the chamber. It the more he sucked, the thicker it got, all until it appeared he had perfectly captured an entire cumulonimbus cloud within this glass object. Tom wasn't sure if it was too much or too little, so once it was solidly white, he removed the bowl and inhaled, a shotgun of smoke absolutely barreling into his mouth. It overwhelmed almost instantaneously, and soon Tom started coughing, small plumes of smoke emerging from his nose and mouth with each passing cough. It felt like his throat was all sorts of scratchy, each cough a little less painful than the last. "Seriously, this is how people get high?" he thought. Slowly, it subsided, and his throat somewhat got back to normal.

It was at that moment that Tom started to feel a weird feeling in his head. It was almost like there was some fuzzy, buzzy part of his brain that was lighting up, like he suddenly felt his synapses getting all excited about something. Then, Tom suddenly just felt ... good. Like, this care- and worry-free kind of good. All the anxieties he had about everything just kind of melted away, and here he was, in this one specific moment, just feeling like everything was just fine. The room took on a very specific contour, the orange light from Matt's single lamp giving everything a warm kind of tone. Tom laid back on Matt's bed, and felt like he could almost sink right into it. The world was suddenly a better place to be in.

"Cluck cluck, motherfuck."

Tom's eyebrows arched: what the fuck was going on? He turned his head and saw ... The Rooster.

Indeed, Matt had donned a costume specifically for the occasion: knee-high yellow soccer socks, neon yellow boxers, and a plastic rooster mask he wore over his face. The rest of his body was exposed, which meant that Tom actually got a nice view of Matt's smooth, muscular stomach and tone arms. His legs still had a decent amount of hair on them, but nothing too out of control. Right now, Matt appeared to be in some sort of sexually dominant form, and seemed to be nothing but pleased with how he looked. Tom kept eying him up and down, completely unsure of how to interpret this vision before him.

"So," started Matt, his voice somewhat muffled by the plastic rooster mask, "are you the footpig everyone's been talking about?"

For some reason, Tom, in this moment, had a hard time discerning what was real. That tingling sensation in his skull was once again manifest, and here, a giant sexy turkey man was giving him orders, and with some great sense of authority as well. The elastics on the knee socks were just a wee bit loose, so they sagged a bit even as Matt stood there, looming over his bed-ridden victim. For some reason, that small detail made things all the hotter. To be totally dominated by a guy dressed up like a fuckin' rooster was ... weirdly hot? Already, Tom could feel the tingles gathering around his privates.

"Are you liking being in my presence, footpig?" the Rooster bellowed.

"Yes, sir," said Tom, meek yet excited at the same time.

"Then why don't you strip for me?"

Almost unconsciously, a wry smirk stretched across Tom's mouth. Oh, this was fun. Without hesitation, Tom took off his shirt, undid his pants belt, toed off his shoes, removed his pants and his socks with it. In less than 20 seconds, he was completely naked in front of the yellow-accented dominant figure before him. The only thing Tom was wearing right now was an ever-thickening boner. Almost instinctively, he was on his knees in front of his new clucking master.

"Very good, boy," said the Rooster in a menacing tone. "I think you deserve a bit of a reward, don't you?"

"Yes sir!" Tom said, enthusiastically.

"Good," Matt replied, "now keep your arms entirely by your side ... and don't fucking move them. Got it?"

"Yes sir," Tom replied, his arms by his side even as his boner was continuing to inflate.

"Now," Matt started, "I think you're going to like this a little bit too much ..."

With that, he raised up his yellow-socked foot and planted it right on Tom's face. The socks obviously hadn't been washed for a bit, so immediately, a warmth and texture filled Tom's senses, the very sweat from Matt's soles lightly dampening Tom's face. His dick immediately twitched in response. Yes: masterful FEET were in his face. This is what he wanted. He wanted so badly to use his arms to grab, feel, and massage those socked wonders before him, but he knew better than to violate master's orders. It was a real struggle keeping his arms like that, and Matt seemed to know that, moving his foot across Tom's face like a windshield wiper, his socked toes stinking up Tom's forehead left to right, right to left. Tom was ecstatic.

Then, Matt lowered his foot down and began playing with Tom's raging footboner, tapping the cockhead with the bottom of his foot, swirling his foot around in a clockwise motion, tormenting Tom's fragile footboner with cotton sensations from all angles.

"Do you like my feet, footpig?" Matt asked.

Tom was sweating right now, denying all his programming to grab his own dick and jerk it to climax, which, he was convinced, was perpetually only five seconds away *if only Matt let him touch it*. He was breaking under horny, stoned duress.

"Yes!" Tom practically screamed.

Matt's foot was continuing to circle around Tom's dick, and it was getting redder and redder with each rotation. All Tom was feeling was the sweaty warmth emanating out from the cotton swirl around on every side of his throbbing member.

"Please," Tom started begging, "I don't know how much more I can take without cumming."

"Awww," said the Rooster, still swirling his foot around as he spoke, "too bad it's me who controls when you cum. You're not gonna cum until I tell you so, aren't you?"

"But sir--" Tom started, his cock twitching against his will now.

"No, you don't get to speak back to me about this issue, boy," Matt stated rather firmly. "You will cum when I give you permission to cum. Now, are you going to be a good little footpig and obey my orders?"

That foot swirled, and Tom's cock was practically throbbing, precum already oozing out and making a steady drizzle onto the floor of Matt's room. He couldn't take it any more, but he knew there was little he could do either.

"Yes sir," Tom said through clenched teeth, "you control when I cum." Tom's body was starting to spasm, barely able to keep in his foothorniness ...

"Good," Matt said, immediately removing his foot away from Tom's cock. Tom started panting, his dick left horny and without sensation all by itself, all of that energy now confusedly finding its way back into his body, leaving Tom in an extremely exasperated state.

Tom tried to collect his bearings, but soon noticed that there was some tenting going on in the yellow boxers that were at his eye level. Matt's hand reached down and tugged on it through the fabric a bit, keeping it warm and excited.

"The fact that there are blowjobs in this world is the very reason why I believe in God," Matt started, tugging on his long member just a bit as he spoke. "You see, it doesn't matter if you're a guy or a girl, but if you're of average height and you get down on your knees, your mouth is perfectly aligned with my cock. It is in the perfect position to swallow it no matter who you are. This was no accident: humans are designed to serve those whom they deem superior. Like, physically designed to suck cock. How fucking awesome is that?"

Tom was not the biggest fan of cocksucking, having never done so before, but even with that, his hazy brain couldn't help but blurt out the inevitable: "So would you like me to suck your cock, sir?"

Although Tom couldn't see behind Matt's rooster mask, he could tell that Matt was grinning in response.

As with most boxers, there was a simple fabric overlay to the slit in the front of them, and Matt didn't have to finagle his member much before his meatrod began sticking out of the front of his boxers, exposed for the wold to see. There it stood, a thick, 8-inch meat popsicle, cut, perfectly rounded and deep pink cockhead, with a smooth shaft of lightly tanned sin where the veins were just visible enough. This was a man who was well-endowed and confidently horny right now. Tom simply stared at it, hypnotized, intrigued by just how ... beautiful it was.

He then tilted his head up to look at the rooster mask staring back at him, and simply asked "So ... what do I do with it?"

"Ha!" chortled the Rooster, "Oh, you are a keeper, you are. Hmm, let's see -- why don't you kiss the tip right there?"

Tom's gaze now focused on the big pink tip that was staring at him. He looked up at the Rooster's face one more time, still unbreaking in its stare, and proceeded to then kiss the tip of the gorgeous cock in front of him. His lips lightly pursed as it touched that orb of meat, and ... it felt OK. Nothing too crazy. It was interesting kissing a part of someone's anatomy, as if thankful for its existence, but, then again, he gladly does the same thing with raw, exposed toes whenever he can, so this seemed about par for the course.

"And again," the Rooster ordered. Tom did so, kissing that pink orb one more time. He could almost see Matt's own cock twitch in appreciation of the gesture, albeit slightly, as it was already at full mast.

"Now, take in the head," Matt ordered.

Tom glanced up at the emotionless Rooster mask, but knew what needed to be done. His mouth opened a bit, and slowly, slid his lips around the tip of Matt's cockhead, the vessel now firmly parked in his mouth. In truth, Tom was a bit unsure as to what to do with it in there, so began swirling his tongue around that valuable cockhead, making sure to moisten up the rim of it as he went.

"Oh yeah," Matt groaned, "this is ... how you do it." Encouraged by the feedback, Tom moved his head a bit closer to Matt's body, sliding a bit more of his member into his mouth, but not too far -- just enough for his tongue to try and slather over it from every possible angle it could. Matt was making light grunting noises as he did so.

Cocksucking really wasn't that bad, Tom thought, as all he did was just take the perky meat in his mouth and slurp, suck, and tease with his tongue. Well, "tease" wasn't the right word -- out-and-out "pleasuring" felt more appropo. Sometimes, with the tight seal his lips had formed around Matt's penis, he could feel the slight bit of throbbing or movement if he found an area that was particularly fertile for his needs. Soon, Tom tried moving his head back and forth and back and forth, creating a real nice pump-and-suck motion on Matt's member, and one Tom kept at a moderate, not frantic pace.

"Fuck, you're being a *great* cocksucker right now, footpig," Matt moaned, and before long, his own voice was getting high pitched. His hands reached down and clenched somewhat tightly into Tom's hair, as if holding on for dear life as he himself came closer and closer to climax.

"Fuck yeah, take it," Matt said, head tilted toward the ceiling, "take my fuckin' load. Obey the fuckin' Rooster, bitch!"

Tom kept his head motion going, and could feel Matt's own cock-a-doodle-doo twitching and then tightening between his lips. Then, it started pulsing, before shooting out gobs upon gobs of hot sticky semen down his throat. Just rope after rope of his hot white seed, all collecting in Tom's throat.

At the moment, Tom was very unsure of how to proceed, so slowly backed his mouth out from Matt's meat, swallowing the semen as soon as he dislodged from the Rooster's member. Matt himself seemed to be in a bit of a daze, still comprehending the orgasm he just experienced.

Meanwhile, Tom was still on his knees, still pretty horny, staring at the monster still-engorged cock sticking out of Matt's yellow boxers. He kept hoping that Matt would soon take off his socks and let him go nuts on his feet, but, even in his hazy stoned mindset, Tom was still at least proud of himself for having conquered a fear he had for some time.

Matt, without saying a word, went and grabbed the bong that Tom had used prior, placed it between his legs, put his mouth over the cylinder, and lit up, creating a nice big ol' cloud of bongsmoke before shotgunning it down his throat. He coughed a bit (and still kept the rooster mask on this whole time), but once the coughs subsided, he placed it to the side and simply laid on his bed, illuminated only by the lamp, seemingly exhausted from what he just experienced. Tom, meanwhile, was still kneeling and naked, unsure of what exactly was going on.

"OK boy," he said, "you've been patient. You can go nuts on my feet. I may pass out, so ya know, keep it in check, OK?"

"Yes sir!" said Tom, a gigantic grin spreading over his face. Stoned and horny as all get out, this was everything Tom wanted: complete and total free reign over a pair of feet he found insanely sexy. He needed no further incentive.

To start, Tom got to the foot of the bed, and simply pressed his mouth and nose deep into the middle of Matt's sweaty socked foot. The smell absolutely shot through his body, and caused him to feel all sorts of horny. It was unlike anything else: every sniff just made his entire body feel good, feel alive, feel submissive and powerful all at once. The aroma of those soles made their way into his skull and painted the word "FEET" on the walls of his cranium. It's all his brain saw, all his brain knew, and all his brain wanted. Tom needed feet right now, and he needed them more than life itself.

He then perched himself up a bit and over to grab on to the elastic band of Matt's right sock, right underneath his knee. He glanced up at Matt, who, still with rooster mask on, seemed to now be in some sort of unshakable trance. He was just ... satisfied, and perhaps close to passing out. So long as he didn't bother him, Tom was beyond OK with proceeding as ordered, slowly pulling that sock down until it was all bunched up around Matt's toes. He didn't remove it quite yet though. Instead, Tom did the same action for Matt's left sock, and pulled it down until it was all bunched up around that set of toes. With Matt's naked heels exposed but his toes covered in scrunched-up rooster socks, Tom felt his own cock twitch in anticipation: it was as if he was making birthday presents for himself, but he didn't dare open them as of yet.

Instead, he kneeled close to the floor, and started slurping at Matt's heels. Even there, despite the thickness of the skin, there was a lot of flavor for his mouth to absorb, and boy howdy did it taste good. He slurped it like a horse trying to wrap its mouth around the corner of a salt lick, and it was full of flavor. He licked and lapped and pumped his dick wildly with his free hand, and felt his entire body be completely overwhelmed with the simple notion that feet ... are fucking amazing. It wasn't his brain that was happy doing this degrading act, no: it was his entire body that was smiling.

Now, Tom was so horny he could take it. With his mouth, he grabbed one ball of scrunched-up rooster sock and dropped it on the floor, doing the same with the other in quick succession. Now, Matt's naked, beautiful, gorgeous straight-boy toes were before him, and they were amazing. There was a light reddening on the heels and the base of his toes (as well as at the tips of them), implying he was on his feet a *lot*. Seeing that sight made him twitch, drool, and pant all the same time. This is what he wanted. Right now, barefoot Matt was just pure sex in his eyes.

Tom's memory of what happened next was a little hazy: all he remembered was greedily working every single inch of his tongue across those soles, in-between those toes, and all over Matt's gorgeous, powerful feet. He chewed on his toehair a bit, slickened up his arches, and those toenails of his practically shined the second they emerged from Tom's hungry mouth. It was almost as if Tom didn't have control over his own body anymore: his fetish was unleashed and it was controlling his every movement and action and Tom himself couldn't be happier.

He didn't quite know how he got in the position, but soon Tom noticed that his body was upright, and his hands were holding Matt's heels right next to his pelvis, and his cock was violently thrusting itself between Matt's perfect soles, giving them all the sexual energy he had. Each thrust felt *good*, each thrust felt *right*, and slowly, with the word "FEET" practically dangling out from Tom's own lips, he shot his load all over the tops of Matt's incredible feet, and they seemed to shoot again and again and again, doubling the load he ingested from Matt earlier. Even the 10th aftershock, depleted in force from the first, was stronger than one of Tom's own masturbation sessions. He came *for* feet, he came *onto* feet, and he came *because* of feet. It was perfect.

"Feet," Tom meekly uttered, as if it's all his brain could comprehend right now.

Tom shook his head, trying to get his bearings a bit. Matt's feet and legs were covered with his sticky, drying cum, but for whatever reason, Tom didn't feel compelled to clean it up. Instead, he heard Matt snoring, his chest rising and falling even with the dumb rooster mask still over his head. Sensing an opportunity to continue on this feeling of foot-aided elation, Tom decided to sit on the corner of the bed, grab that bong, and take one more hit. The bowl was mostly cached out, so Tom didn't get as much smoke as he did before, but he got a decent cloud trapped inside, and got a decent inhale off of it. This might be all he needed to get through the rest of the night. Yeah, feet. Feet were great. This is all he needed to know. Tom put on his pants and shirt but simply carried his shoes and socks in his hand. He swiped Matt's bunched up yellow rooster socks, caked in his masculine musk, and tucked them deep down into his own shoes so he could make his way back to his room without anyone wondering what he's doing. He exited Matt's room and quietly closed the door behind him.

Tom snuck barefoot across the wood-paneled floor of the frat, passing some guys but, as was proving to the the usual case, all of them didn't pay him much of any mind. As he got to the first floor and eventually to the door of Bobby's room, that second wave of high suddenly struck him, and as he opened the door, everything once again felt just ... wonderful ...

CHAPTER EIGHT: Found Out

Bobby was again not home, but due to the pot leaving Tom feeling more lucid and languid than normal, he tossed his shoes and socks over to his sleeping area and actually sat down on Bobby's bed, trying to get his bearings. He looked across the room to Bobby's dormant computer, but given how lucid he was feeling, Tom leaned back a bit, propping his head up against the wall of the room, mulling over and somewhat digesting what just happened. His head was now foggy with bongsmoke but it really didn't matter all that much: as of now, all that just happened with the mysterious Rooster Man seemed part of some surreal, hazy dream. He didn't know much that came out of it, but he did know that feet were feet and feet feet feet -- oh god, it's starting again.

Despite having just unleashed a monster load all over the Rooster's naked soles and his dick practically begging for mercy, Tom couldn't help himself, and his idle hands wandered over to his crotch, feeling his shaft and balls up a bit while he thought about just how utterly great and wonderful male feet were. No, really, they were fantastic objects of worship and desire. They needed to be treated and tended to at all hours of the day if they knew what was good for them. Tom kind of took a step back mentally, realizing that male feet were now basically echoing out to him, calling him, summoning him to some higher purpose. A weird bit of existential dread kind of crept in as well, as if to insinuate that there may be more to life than this, but what if Tom's mind and desires really lead to him becoming a grade-A footpig and little else? It was a strangely scary proposition, and one he wasn't ready to deal with yet. Tom needed a distraction to somewhat get him "back on track" in terms of feeding his foot fetish, 'cos even as he was already at a bit of a wobbly half-mast, he needed to strengthen that sensation all the more.

He looked around the room, looking for some sort of stimuli, and then, of course, his eyes spotted something on the ground: that pair of Bobby's used white socks. Despite his claim the night before that he was hiding all of his socks from the self-admitted footslave, there were still a few pairs that were littered about the floor -- organization wasn't really Bobby's strong suit. However, here in front of Tom was a pair so succinct, so beautiful, and so lightly dirty with gray impressions he couldn't help but be intrigued all over again. Tom got up out of the sitting position he was in on the bed (which was a pain, he should add, 'cos that bong smoke didn't make him want to get up or go anywhere), and immediately plopped himself on the floor on all fours, like a dog, savoring the sight in front of him: genuine, used Bobby socks. He was getting really turned on right now, not only by the prospect of getting to sniff the socks of a straight dom such as this, but also because, well, it was just so *wrong.* Tom felt like he was doing something genuinely out of line, taking a bite out of forbidden fruit as it were, and, really, the simple act of doing it was nothing less than exhilarating. He crawled forward until his face was was no less than a foot away from Bobby's socks, and already he felt his dick a-twitchin'. His brain was firing off all the electricity it could muster at the prospect of such excitement; truly, Tom was coming into his own as a footpig.

His nose drew closer, and it was definitely within sniffing distance. Being as uninhibited as he was, Tom just went in and pressed his nose squarely into Bobby's socks as they laid there and just inhaled.

Holy fuck.

It was hard to define the exact scent which Tom was taking in at this moment, but Tom was knocked out flat by it. It was pungent, potent, a bit cheesy, a bit sweaty, and just absolutely dripping with masculinity. It was every bit of olfactory goodness that could ever be created condensed down into the greatest goddamn smell that Tom had ever had the chance to intake. It filled his lungs, spread through his veins, and controlled his body in a matter of seconds. It was ... fantastic. His cock immediately went to full-mast, and in the drug-addled haze that everything was in, Tom couldn't stop himself: he pulled down his pants, whipped out his ever-stiffening footboner, and put one sock to his nostril and dragged the other one over his genitals, under the balls and around the base of his shaft, inhaling one sock while teasing his own member with the other, putting each end of his body at the complete control and whim of Bobby's foot musk.

Christ, what a feeling, having the essence of Bobby's bare feet control his body, sending him into a lusty overdrive that was unlike anything he had ever experienced. He was being such a naughty boy, but man, inhaling that scent from Bobby's socks was unlike anything else he had ever experienced. Each inhale made his dick twitch in tandem, forever linking the two acts together until they became nothing more than a simple Pavlovian response. Those electric buzzy feelings at the tip of his cock were getting more and more prominent, the feeling of Bobby's sock fabric dragging across his ballsac amplifying the sensation tenfold, his entire essence being completely and totally overwhelmed by the thought of Bobby's smelly feet. Oh god, here it was, he was gonna cum again ...

The door to the room opened. Tom turned his head seconds before cumming, and saw Bobby's naked feet in slip-on sandals inches away from him. Those toes had such a meaty, powerful splay, lightly tan from being outdoors, and seeing that image this close to climax simply burned their way into Tom's footpig brain, the tingling sensation to the point where he can't control it, and--

Tom came. Despite having already blown so much on Matt's feet, the stoned little footpig was humiliated beyond all words, cumming to Bobby's socks while staring at Bobby's sandaled toes while Bobby simply stood there, no doubt aghast and disgusted by what he was seeing. After that first euphoric rope of cum shot out of him, the degradation seeped in way too deep, and Tom felt lower than he ever had in his entire life.

"What," the bearded, T-shirt-and-shorts-wearing Bobby started, "the fuck."

Tom was in the absolutely unenviable position of trying to clean himself up a bit while he addressed this matter head on -- setting the sock he was sniffing down but soon realizing the one near his crotch actually got some of his seed on it.

"I can explain--" started Tom, realizing that those were probably the three worst words he could say in a situation like this, zipping up his pants as he did so.

"No, there is nothing to explain!" shouted Bobby, visibly livid. "Ya know, I was being the reasonable one by letting your freakish impulses stay with me but I only did so under the idea that you were going to fucking contain your goddamn urges while you were here. I was doing *you* a favor. I was doing *them* a favor. Goddammit, its' the same damn thing every fucking time."

"Bobby--" Tom started.

"Just ... just clean yourself up," Bobby said with a resigned tone before powering on his computer. Tom sheepishly got himself up, left the socks on the floor, and made his way out to the frat's nearby bathroom.

As Tom scrubbed his hands free of cum in the bathroom sink, he began quietly cursing himself, questioning just how stupid he could be, biting the hand that feeds him, of not having basic respect or control. Bobby was weirdly nice to him in comparison to the other frat dudes that were hanging around, and doing this felt like a violation of this trust. Hell, Tom was just downright mortified by what just happened. He knew he was better than that, but the bong hit and his overzealous horniness simply made it so that all he could do was just ... give in to his sad, sad temptation. He felt like such an idiot. He really, really didn't want to go back into that room because he was already so embarrassed -- hell, if he could, he would run off campus and never return if that was an option. Then, he remembered that contract. That dangling, evil contract that he signed with his own hand that made sure he wasn't going to go anywhere for a long while, 'lest his social life and any potential employers he ever has get a glimpse of his foot-obsessive ways. He was genuinely distraught at the moment, but knew that the only way to get through this was to move forward. He dried off his hands and made his way back to Bobby's room.

As he creaked the door open, Bobby was sitting at his computer, amply checking some sort of news website that Tom didn't recognize. Bobby didn't even acknowledge that Tom had entered the room, as the self-professed footpig simply made his way back to his sleeping area on the floor. He got out his own laptop and began opening up some emails, checking his Facebook, etc. The two boys were simply tapping and clicking away at their computers deep in the night, neither acknowledging the other as best they could. The air was thick with an unspoken tension. Tom nervously glanced over at Bobby just ... well, just 'cos. He felt like he was walking on thin ice at the moment, and didn't want to disturb the natural order of where things were.

Then, out of nowhere, Bobby turned to Tom, still in his sandals and shorts, and began speaking: "I guess the hardest thing for me is just figuring out what the fuck your endgame here is. OK. Listen: I'm really pissed off at you, which is a real rarity for me 'cos I'm not one to get pissed off at people very often, if ever. I felt like you and I just ... I don't know, that we had some sort of unspoken agreement and you went ahead and violated it."

"I know--" started Tom.

"Please," Bobby interrupted, "let me finish. I guess I just ... I don't know. That's a really fucking weird thing to walk into, man. And, you know, I try to be the pacifist here and really imagine what other people are going through, but I just don't get it, ya know. I mean, why feet? Why can't you just, I dunno, contain it for more appropriate times? And, most of all, why my goddamn socks? Was it just 'cos they were there or what?"

"I mean," Tom stammered, "it's just, I mean, I dunno -- your feet are ... attractive, Bobby."

"OK, now I *know* you're lying to me," Bobby said, a bit of anger in his voice.

"But I'm not!" Tom said, a bit defiant. "Your feet are ... fucking great. They are ... sublime. They are attractive. I know you might just, I dunno, disregard them 'cos you don't give them much mind, but, you gotta understand, wearing sandals, showing off your feet like that -- it's a mindset, and not everyone immediately subscribes to it, I know, but whether or not you know it, your feet are objectively attractive. Having a foot fetish myself, I dunno -- maybe it's my job to really readjust things or put them in their proper order in a more universal sense, but I will out and out acknowledge feet that are attractive, and like it or not, your feet are. There, I said it. They're great."

Bobby had his eyebrow arched slightly, staring at him in disbelief. "Dude," he started, "if you like my feet then, ya know, hey, that's great. I can accept that. But I fucking *hate* having my own feet touched. Like, really."

"But why?" Tom countered, inquisitively.

"I mean, do I have to give a reason?" Bobby started. "Like, I mean, they're just feet, you know? There's nothing special about 'em. Fuck if I know what you see in them, but, and forgive me for being a bit bold here, but whatever you see you're just projecting. Like, really. It's not even supposed to be a thing, and yet it is for you."

Maybe there was some strange spiritual confidence that was about in the air, or maybe it was just the impulsive need to lash out against someone that was ragging on his own belief system, but the shame that had been dripping from Tom's person instantly dried up as he stood up to face Bobby.

"Get on that bed," Tom ordered.

"What? No!" Bobby countered.

"Bobby, we are going to resolve this once and for all, OK?" Tom said, an air of authority to what he was saying.

"Dude, I'm already sick of talking about feet, OK? Can you just drop it?" Bobby asked.

"No," said Tom, still staunch in his position. "You're going to get on that bed right now, and we're not going to simply stop talking about this issue for the night -- we're going to resolve this once and for all, OK?"

Bobby audibly sighed, realizing that this might be the only way to shut Tom up. "OK, fine," he said, walking over to his bed, stepping out of his sandals, and flopping down so he was resting on top of his sheets, head on his pillow.

"Good," Tom said, walking over and sitting on the end of Bobby's bed, his back against the wall, his lap perpendicular to Bobby's legs. "Now put your feet up here."

"Ugh, really?" Bobby intoned.

"You want to get this over and done with once and for all, right?" asked Tom, coyly.

Bobby audibly sighed again. He put his bare feet right into Tom's lap.

"I won't lie, Tom -- I'm a bit scared by what's going to happen next."

"Don't worry," Tom said, "I'm going to walk you through this very simply, very slowly. There's no way this won't feel a bit weird at first, but I'm asking you to trust me, OK?"

"Whatever," Bobby said, pressing his head even further into his pillow and closing his eyes, as if hoping that he'll just wake up out of this at some point.

Tom realized this so knew he had to work whatever magic he could. In some ways, Tom had no idea what he was doing, but his confidence so far had managed to get Bobby's bare feet right there in his lap, so he wasn't going to squander this opportunity at any cost.

Tom placed one hand on each foot, carefully. He didn't move his hands, but just kept them there. Already, he could feel Bobby's feet tensing up a bit. "See," Tom started, "all I'm doing is putting my hands on your feet. I'm not doing anything to them at all whatsoever. Just ... just feel that for a second, and realize nothing is going to happen."

Tom looked over and saw Bobby's face somewhat turned into a bit of grimace. It was a faint one, but he was really righting the sensations that he was experiencing right now. Tom smirked a bit, because he had the feeling that he had Bobby exactly where he wanted him.

"Very good, Bobby," he said, feeling those feet relax slightly after about a solid minute. "See? I said I wasn't going to do anything and I haven't. All I did was just make sure that your feet are relaxed, comfortable, and used to the feeling of my hands on them. Are you feeling comfortable?"

"Reasonably," he replies.

"OK, then if you wouldn't mind, I'm going to massage them for just a bit now, OK? I'll be real gentle," Tom promised.

There was a bit of a pause as Bobby seemed to mull this prospect over and said "Um, OK."

Tom needed no further encouragement. He began using his thumbs to start feeling out the base of Bobby's toes, rubbing them gently but firmly, actually trying to feel the knots that were inside and actually doing something about them. Bobby's face again cringed, keeping his arms close to his chest, but that stopped after a bit. Tom wound up narrowing in on a knot right near the top of his instep that he carefully felt, massaged, and smoothed out. Bobby's shoulders and face relaxed somewhat. It's as if he suddenly realized that Tom's intentions were actually not cruel in scope at all: he genuinely was trying to work the knots out and make him feel better. This was new to Bobby because, quite frankly, he never experienced this before.

Tom, of course, was feeling something else entirely different. To feel Bobby's warm soles between his fingers was nothing short of electrifying. He was seriously considering changing over to become a theatre major at this moment because right now feeling Bobby's toes was causing him to get harder than he's ever been, his dick practically straining out of his pants, and yet somehow he was maintaining a cool, professional air about this. He was not opposed to this feeling of all, of running his fingertips up and over every inch of Bobby's sexy bare size 8.5 feet, each new inch of footflesh sending all sorts of jitters and shivers through his body. Tom couldn't help himself but did everything he could to maintain the guise of a regular person: right now, touching Bobby's feet was his entire world.

"You feeling better?" Tom said, keeping one eye on Bobby's more relaxed face and another on the shape of his glorious, meaty toes.

"Yeah," Bobby said, resigned, "I mean ... I just haven't ever gotten a foot massage before, ya know?"

"Which is a shame," Tom interjected, "'cos you have some really nice feet."

"Guy," Bobby started, "my feet are not sexy. They're just feet, OK. Boxy, sweaty ... feet, ya know? There's nothing that special about them."

"Are you joking?" Tom asked with an unusual pointedness. "Dude, your feet are just ... great to look at. I mean, really truly. The shape of your toes is lengthy and the splay on them is surprisingly enticing. Your soles are warm and have perfect shading on them. Your arches too are firm but not too egregious, as they're--"

"Dude," Bobby interrupted, "how many other parts of my feet can you actually describe? I mean, like, really. I don't think there's anything else you can--"

"Would you care for me to go on?" Tom asked coyly.

There was a heavy pause in the room. Bobby opened his eyes to see Tom staring at him with his own feet in his hands. Here he was, trusting the footpig to rub his feet, not too long after he caught him jerking off to his dirty socks, and all Tom was doing was complimenting every aspect of his feet. It was unlike anything he had ever experienced before. Bobby was probably the last one to indulge in this bizarre fantasy that Red, Matt, and the other guys were concocting, but right now, perhaps because Tom had so diligently worked to get that knot out, he was, against all odds, partially convinced as to what he was saying.

"My feet *are* sexy, aren't they?" Bobby said.

"Oh fuck," Tom replied, "like you have no idea."

"Have you been ... crushing on my feet for some time?" Bobby asked.

"To be honest," Tom said, "like you wouldn't believe. They are so meaty and so tasty and so desirous. There is a long list of things I would give up just for the chance to put your prehensile toes right in my mouth. I know the sensation would be undeniably weird at first, but to have someone worshiping your body like this, to be feeding it so much love and affection -- it really is unlike anything else you've experienced. Obviously, I won't do anything ever without your consent but, I don't know -- you strike me as the guy who would be up for doing at least one new thing in his life if not just for the fact that he could say that he did it."

Again, the room filled with silence. Tom looked over to see Bobby, eyes open, mulling this prospect. Tom was actually getting nervous as each second rolled by without a response from the man whose bare feet he was cradling right now in his arms.

"You know what?" Bobby started, "You may have convinced me. I don't want you to get too sexual or anything--"

"Oh no, I wouldn't dare!" Tom interjected.

"Yeah," Bobby continued, "I walked in on you, remember. Well, I mean, yeah, YOLO and all that nonsense. Just ... ya know, start gently. We'll just keep this up until I'm done with it, OK?"

Tom had the biggest, goofiest grin spread across his face. "You got it, sir!"

With that, Tom repositioned himself where he could bend over and have his mouth directly above Bobby's toes. They twitched slightly being in the presence of his warm breath, but that's exactly what Tom needed to see: each toe an active creature responsive to sensation. Smirking a bit, Tom wrapped his mouth around Bobby's meaty index toe, and gave it a good long slurp, his mouth around the base of it before slowly pulling up, sucking all of the flavor he possibly could of it.

Feeling that toe inside his mouth was unlike anything else Tom had ever experienced. He placed all four of Bobby's smaller toes in his mouth and sucked and licked, and it was amazing feeling his toes somewhat recoil and to a small degree get into the sensations as well, as those mantoes were experiencing true worship for what was proving to be their first time ever. They were almost quivering with sensation, overwhelmed by Tom's mouth, eager tongue, and horny saliva all hitting them at once. However, if Tom was blessed with anything resembling footpig intuition, it was definitely kicking in now, as he could tell, for whatever reason, that Bobby, against all odds, was actually enjoying having his feet serviced. Tom had no hard facts proving this, but he just felt it in his bones, and it was ... immensely satisfying.

Of course, as the course in administering proper footpig duties, Tom then proceeded to warp his mouth around Bobby's big toe, and just sucked it up and down, up and down, up and down, not unlike a sensuous blowjob. Tom noticed that Bobby was squirming a bit due to this action, but in the good way: the sensation was pleasurable to him. Noticing this, Tom immediately switched up his technique, lifting up Bobby's other foot, and, in a moment of passion, just dragging his tongue around his thick heel and then dragging it up across his sole and then slurping the smelly, warm base of Bobby's toes. Bobby gasped a bit at this, but that only egged Tom to go on further, as he did another heel-to-toes lick, finishing by individually sucking each and every toe in a thorough manner, slithering his tongue in-between them causing some actual genuine tickles to shoot through Bobby's body.

"Stop!" Bobby playfully cried out.

Tom grinned, and proceeded to lickle the foot some more, his serpentine tongue writhing in-between Bobby's toes time and time time again, up to the point where Bobby was trying to pull his foot away but Tom's firm grip prevented him from doing so. Bobby's other foot was pressing into Tom's side to try and peel the eager mouth off but Tom simply switched his attention at that point and began assaulting Bobby's other foot with his tongue, focusing not just on those toes but also dabbing his tonguetip all over Bobby's sole, furiously licking his arches just to elicit a high-pitched giggle out of the boy. Tom was genuinely enjoying this role, and, despite now having cum twice in the past few hours, his dick was once again at full mast, physically drained but unable to fight off the desirable sensations of having those feet fill up his brain's pleasure center like there was no tomorrow.

"OK, that's enough!" Bobby said, still laughing but with a bit of earnestness in his voice. Tom knew that Bobby actually meant it, so released his grip of Bobby's feet. Bobby recoiled a bit and was in a bit of a lazy fetal position, but was still smiling.

"So," Tom started, "do you have to begrudgingly admit that that was kind of fun?"

"Isn't there a clause in your contract that maintains that you can't tell anyone about the things you do within the walls of this house?" Bobby asked, half-jokingly.

"Um, I don't think so," Tom said, "but I could whip out my copy to check."

"Well," Bobby continued, "regardless, I got to get to bed, and I think it goes without saying that you don't mention this to anyone -- not even Red, OK?"

"Yeah, I can do that," Tom replied. Before long, Bobby picked up his toothbrush and worked his way over to the bathroom, which Tom soon followed in suit. As they both brushed their teeth in the bathroom mirror, Tom's eyes kept glancing down and the very desirous sight of Bobby's bare feet standing on the cool tile of the bathroom floor, but never made his glances too overt -- although after all the two young men had just been through, Bobby may have been able to figure that out on his own.

They went back to Bobby's room -- fuck knows what hour of the morning it was at this point -- and Bobby took off his shirt, revealing a bit of a paunch belly that was still kind of sexy in its own way, and then crawled under his sheets. Tom likewise undressed and laid down in his designated sleeping space, very content. Now with all the lights and Bobby's computer monitor off, Tom could see a few rays of moonlight stretch into the room, and Tom was very much at peace.

"Hey," Bobby said in a quiet tone to the darkened room, "thanks for that. It was strangely fun ..."

"Anytime," Tom reflexively said, delighted by that kind of affirmation. With that, he nuzzled up to his pillow made out of strewn-about clothes, and, with his veins pumping more exhaustion than there was blood, Tom instantly conked out to sleep.

CHAPTER NINE: Preston

Tom awoke as sunlight was baking itself into his face, and he immediately rolled over to cover his eyelids with a discarded T-shirt (whether it was his or Bobby's, he didn't really care all that much). However, the warmth of the light was enough to slowly stir him awake, and Tom reluctantly rose into a state of actual consciousness. His eyes flickered a bit, and he then was able to see the rays illuminate the dusty room all its own. He groggily lifted up his head and noticed that Bobby was nowhere to be seen: he must've headed out to classes or breakfast or something. However, there was something a bit off about the way the light coming in: the position of the sun seemed a bit high. Tom haphazardly flapped his arm around, looking for his phone, found it, and turned the screen on to reveal it was ... 11:24am.

Well fuck.

Throughout all the commotion of everything that happened yesterday, he must've forgotten to turn on his alarm for his classes. However, Tom felt ... strangely unconcerned with this development. After all, he had already missed about three of them and he was on a bit of a foot-high from all his proclivity activities from the day before, so ... fuck it. He was accidentally playing hooky from class for the day, so you might as well enjoy it, right? After all, he's got friends who could email him notes later (perhaps some of them would enjoy a nice ol' bit of worship as payment, ay?), so why not just take a "mental health" day? Had a nice ring to it and everything.

Tom wound up wondering around the Frat for a bit, amazed at just how empty the thing was. Perhaps he shouldn't have been -- his impressions of frats for the longest time was just a very bro-centric culture that was all testosterone and beer pong, but all of them were seriously studying quite hard for their degrees. It wasn't as much a frat as it was a ghost town. Tom made his way to the kitchen area, and noticed there was a box of (of course) Wheaties on the top of the fridge. Tom found a (relatively) clean bowl in the cupboards and poured some milk into it. He emptied out what was left of the Wheaties, tossed it in the trash, grabbed a (relatively) clean spoon, and made his way back to his room. He opened up his laptop and wound up loading up an episode of *Lost* he hadn't seen, and had a morning that was reminiscent of Saturday mornings: barefoot in pajama pants and a T-shirt, eating cereal while watching cartoons (or, in this case, a CGI smoke monster). Really, Tom was in a genuinely great mood.

After the episode wrapped up (and his head was filled with more questions than answers from the *Lost* episode), he picked up his bowl and made his way back to the kitchen to put his bowl in the sink, as he did so, there was a tall guy there whom Tom hadn't seen before. The man was, like, tall tall, like 6'4" maybe? Maybe a bit taller? He was pretty lanky as well, short dark hair and thick black-rimmed glasses -- he looked like a classic geek/nerd but with a stature that dwarfed over all. Most of all, though, was the thing that made Tom notice him in the first place: sticking out of those dark blue jeans were some rather large, lengthy feet resting in some monster cheap blue flip-flops. It looks like he got a half-size too big at an Old Navy sale, but, strangely, they were complementing his frame to a T. He seemed to be inspecting something in the fridge, but, being as he wasn't involved in the entire contract-based setup that Tom was in, Tom didn't make any effort to contact him, simply putting the bowl in the sink and then making his way out.

No less than two steps out of the kitchen he heard a voice come from the kitchen: "Hey! You!"

Tom froze in his tracks and turns around: the tall, lanky, flip-flopped god stood before him, wearing an unzipped red hoodie over a novelty T-shirt that advertised Moog synthesizers. Were it not for the fact that his voice sounded a bit intimidating right now, Tom would be completely swept up in the total package that was this gargantuan dream boat (with gargantuan feet to boot). As of now, he was a bit frightened at the figure staring down at him.

"Did you eat my Wheaties?" he asked.

"Um, yes," Tom meekly replied. "Was ... was that yours?"

"As a matter of fact it was, son," the man replied, "and I'm a little cheesed that you just went and ate them. Hell, it's not even the fact that you ate them -- it's more the fact that you didn't even ask permission first. Had you done so, perhaps we ..."

The man didn't finish his sentence. He simply stared at Tom's shy, guilty face, and cocked his head, as if trying to recognize him.

"You're not a member of this frat, are you?" the man asked.

"No, I'm not," Tom replied, looking down (at the guy's feet in flips).

"You're ... you're the foot guy, aren't you?" the man continued.

"Yes, I am," Tom said, now looking at some random point on the hardwood floor so as not to make it seem like he was staring at the man's feet.

"Oh, this is fucking golden," the guy started, "oh, I have been curious about this since I heard about this but man, this is great. I'm Preston, by the way."

"And I'm--"

"And you're BITCH, if you know what's good for you," Preston said in a surprisingly menacing tone. Tom was legitimately frightened right now.

Preston walked by him and went right into the main lounging room, saying "follow me" as he walked, the sound of those cheap blue flips slapping against the bottom of his heel with each step signaling Tom's ever-descending journey into the mindset of a true submissive. As utterly frightened as he was right now, Tom was also, perhaps unsurprising given everything he's been through, a bit turned on.

Preston sat on the couch in the main living room, afternoon sun pouring in, and he crossed his legs, his left over his right, leaving one sandaled foot right there for Tom to survey and admire.

"Ya know, I don't know what the fuck you and the guys created with your whole foot slavery thing, but just 'cos you ate my goddamn cereal, I think we should give this a test drive. I mean, per your little contract thing, I believe I can be designated as a god worthy of your admiration, no?"

"You're right," Tom said, timidly.

"Good," Preston continued, "and, you being a good little footpig, are going to do exactly what I say, right?"

"Yes," Tom nodded, still unable to get over the fact that the tall nerd with the massive feet in the cheap blue sandals was ordering him around so suddenly. Did he have a target on his head that just read "Order Me Around" or something?

"Then why don't you go over to that endtable over there and get me a blue marker from that drawer?" Preston ordered.

"OK," Tom said, taking one step before he was interrupted--

"On all fours, I should mention," Preston noted.

Tom did as he was told and, still in his T-shirt and pajama pants, got on his hands and knees and made his way over to the endtable. It was a small wooden thing with a single drawer on it, a big ol' wooden knob there to pull it open. Tom reached for it and--

"No!" Preston shouted. "Not with your hand! Open it with your mouth like the fuckin' footpig you are!"

This was escalating quickly.

Tom did as he ordered, and put the wooden knob of the endtable drawer in his mouth and used his neck to help pull it open. Not needing to be yelled at again, Tom went over to the side of the opened drawer and stuck his face in, finding a blue Sharpie marker in there but made sure to grab it with just his mouth. It took him a few slobbery tries, but he finally managed to put the marker in his mouth. He pulled it out of the drawer and then used his nose to push the drawer closed. He then started crawling his way back to Preston on his hands and knees. At this point, Preston had pulled out his iPhone and appeared to be filming it.

"Oh man," he started, "this is just too great. I mean, like, you have no idea. Yeah, crawl to me, boy."

Tom finally got up the point there he was just a few inches away from Preston's crossed, sandaled foot.

"I'll take that please, thank you," Preston said, reaching down for the marker and pull it from Tom's mouth. "Eww, slobber!" he noted, holding the marker by the tip and then drying it off on Tom's shirt. "Much better."

As he did this, Tom couldn't help but stare the the bony, long, sexy toes that were right there in front of him. There was a small bit of redness to the tips of the toes and the ball of the foot as far as Tom could see, meaning that young Preston here walked around in his flips a *lot*, which was only ramping up Tom's excitement even more, up to the point where it was winning out over the feelings of powerless terror he felt being at Preston's command.

"Now tell me," Preston started, waving the marker around in one hand in a teasing fashion while trying to hold his iPhone camera steady in the other, trained in carefully on Tom's eager face, "would you like to kiss my toes, footpig?"

"Yes!" Tom said a bit too enthusiastically.

"Ha!" Preston chortled, "Oh man, it's almost too easy with you, isn't it? OK, and would you be willing to sacrifice, say, your humility in order to have the absolute honor of kissing my huge size 13s?"

Tom grimaced a bit, but wordlessly nodded in response.

"Then why don't you lean in a bit, close your eyes, and tell me what you like about my feet while I draw on your forehead, OK?"

Tom didn't like this. He could deal with the humiliation of being in a room with Matt and Dave and Red and dealing with their demands and threats of public exposure but this was different. Preston was a variable he had not counted on in any way whatsoever. Here was a guy who was just having a lot of fun right now, humiliating Tom by making a video of him at his submissive best, and under no specific means tied to the contract. Preston could release this thing on his Facebook within 30 minutes for all Tom knew, and having an element of "uncontrollable danger" like this was not something he was entirely stoked about.

However, given the circumstances, he already had video him crawling on all fours with a pen in his mouth, and any defiance of his orders may provoke him to release that video sooner than later. Fearing he had no better option, Tom closed his eyes and moved his head forward until it was resting on Preston's jean-covered leg, and began speaking freely:

"The thing I love most about your feet from looking at them is just how long they are. I love the length of your toes 'cos that means they have a really really good splay, which means that looking at the pinky toe when it's all spread out just must make it look like a thing of glory. The way your toes are bony is cute, the way there kind of curves to them, like ..."

Tom kept going on as he felt the tip of the marker being pressed onto his forehead. Given how one of Preston's hands was already holding the iPhone, the free-form hand was a bit clumsy (or at least felt that way) in drawing ... whatever it was drawing, but Tom simply ignored those sensations as he kept on going on about how hot he thought Preston's massive feet were.

"... and I love the way that the sandals you have are, like, a half-size too big as if the plate the meal is on is so big you just look at the meal as that much more appetizing and--"

"OK," Preston interjected, "that's enough there, footpig." Tom tossed the marker near to where that endtable was but without much regard for where it landed.

"Now," Preston continued, "I really like what I wrote on your face, but you're not allowed to remove it until midnight tonight, got it?"

"Yes sir," Tom said, begrudgingly acknowledging the hard truth of the matter.

"Now, you *really* want to kiss my feet now, don't ya?" Preston started.

"Yes sir," Tom replied, honest as ever.

"Well why don't you start by kissing the bottom of my sandals here?"

Tom was about to say "yes" but his lips simply took over and moved directly into kissing position. Fortunately, despite being Preston's primary mode of transportation, Preston's flip-flops weren't all that dirty, but Tom knew it wasn't about the actual act of kissing them that made them what they were: it was what doing so represented. It wasn't the fact that Tom was kissing the lowest part of his new master -- it was the fact he was kissing the lowest part of what his master's lowest part actually stands on. It was rough. Tom was doing it, but not loving it.

"OK, that was just appetizers," Preston noted, now planting both sandaled feet on the hardwood floor. "Now, footpig, you have permission to kiss my toes. Go to town on them -- now!"

Tom needed no further encouragement: he practically dropped to the ground and began kissing each toe emphatically and with much gusto. He kissed the pinky then the ring then the middle then the index then the big then the other big then ... it kept up like this. Tom could actually hear Preston snidely guffaw as he rabidly, furiously kissed the feet of the lanky lord who was now making him serve.

"Hey," Preston said, "look up."

Tom did so, and saw Preston's iPhone practically in his face.

"What are you?" Preston goaded.

"I'm ... I'm a footpig?" Tom said.

"Noooo," Preston drew out, menacingly, "you're *my* footpig, got it?"

"I'm your footpig sir," Tom said.

"Good!" Preston said, "and now everytime I ask you, I want you to look up and tell me that, OK? Can you do that for me footpig?"

"Yes sir," Tom said.

"Good -- now get back to work."

Tom immediately bent back down and continued kissing the tops of Preston's toes with passion and fury. Preston would sometimes wiggle or scrunch his toes just to keep Tom's approach fresh, but he was clearly enjoying teasing the living hell out of his trained toe-kisser.

"What are you?" Preston asked.

Tom looked up to the camera: "I'm your footpig, sir."

"Good boy!" Preston said. And with that, Tom got down and kept on kissing those toes as they stuck out of those flip-flops, Tom even managing to whiff a bit of scent out of them as well. "What are you?" Preston asked again. And again, Tom looked up, giving the same reply, before going back down.

This happened about five more times -- each one greeted by Preston's impish squeal of glee -- before Preston audibly groaned: "Oh man! It looks like the space for new video ran out. Eyes up here, footpig."

Tom lifted up his head.

"Since I'm not getting any video of you," Preston stated, "you don't get any more toes, understood?"

"Yes sir," Tom said, a bit saddened as he was really getting into that.

"Well, who knows footpig, I might just be benevolent and let you watch that video sometime -- or maybe I'll be super-nice and not let that video see the eyes of all my Facebook friends. How nice would that be, footpig?"

"It would be nice, sir," Tom noted.

"Good. Now, I'm about to head back to my room, but you can't get up until I'm upstairs, OK?"

"Got it, sir," Tom said.

"And, just so you don't forget how all this started ... you're going to get me a nice new box of Wheaties by the time I wake up tomorrow morning, right?" Preston leered.

"Yes, sir," Tom said.

"Good boy," Preston said, rather gleeful. "Well you just think about what you did as me and these feet you kissed so much work their way back to their domain ..."

Preston walked off, the sound of those sandals slapping his heels once again, leaving Tom on the floor, horny and anxious. When he heard the door close to a room upstairs, Tom got up off the floor and made his way to the bathroom. Although the way he was viewing it was backwards, he could clearly make out the words "PRESTON'S FOOTPIG" written on his forehead in big blue letters. Tom realized he better go out now to get that box of cereal ... but then remembered that Preston ordered him to not wipe those letters from his forehead either ... which means he'd have to go out in public with that written on him. Fuck. His initial idea to go to the on-campus store was immediately squashed in favor of going to the small mini-mart off campus, dealing with the stares of strangers instead of those of classmates. Tom sighed about this, but knew what had to be done for the sake of the rest of his humility.

He got on some regular street clothes (overshirt, jeans, shoes & socks) and made his way out the door of the frat, walking through every backalley he could think of to get off campus without being spotted by a classmate. He finally got to the mini-mart and went in without making eye-contact with anyone, but still scanning to see if there were any faces he knew. Fortunately there weren't. He found a box of Wheaties and went to the checkout counter, laying out a $5 bill and, again, not making eye contact with the clerk.

As the clerk handed off the change to Tom, he asked "Hey man -- what's that on your forehead?"

Tom wasn't exactly sure how to react, so simply said "Pledge week, man -- every frat's gotta have them."

"Well good luck to you then!" the clerk shouted. Tom thanked him and scurried off as quickly as he could back to the frat.

This was supposed to be a simple "mental health" day, but after this and the looming prospect of being at Red's mercy for the night ... Tom knew he was in for something absolutely terrifying.

+ + +

Tom passed the rest of the day doing what he knew best: gathering homework from classmates, looking up study materials on his various syllabuses, and doing whatever classes were good enough to have online quizzes be a part of the final score. He excelled at all these things, but every once in while, coming across a hard math problem, he'd inadvertently scratch his forehead, as if trying to rub out some reasoning. When he brought his hand down, he noticed a smudge of blue marker across his forefinger, a reminder of Preston's oh-so-casual and oh-so-devious dominance. It really sucked not being able to wipe this from his forehead, but Tom knew full well that it was better to submit than it was to get punishments with that level of ... severity to them.

As he worked through his problems, he lost complete lack of time, up to the point where Bobby walked in the door at around 4:45pm in shorts, those slip-on sandals, and a hoodie (what a hipster), backpack slung over his shoulder.

"What's shakin' there, Tom?" Bobby started, as talkative as Tom's ever seen him. "You seemed to be sleeping pretty *what the fuck is on your forehead?*"

"Well," Tom started, "it's kind of obvious, isn't it? I ate Preston's Wheaties."

"Yeah," Bobby agreed, staring in disbelief at Tom's forehead, "but, I mean, he's not really a part of that whole deal. How did he ... I mean, what happened?"

"I ate his Wheaties not knowing they were his," Tom started, "and when I was returning my bowl he kind of put two and two together and realized I was the guy who signed the contract so pretty much just made me ... dance for his amusement."

"Dance?" Bobby asked.

"Well, do humiliating things," Tom clarified. "I mean, he *did* make me kiss the tops of his toes, which was really pretty hot, but he also took a video of me doing it with his iPhone, so, I dunno, I guess I have to be on my best behavior around him."

"No you don't," Bobby said. "I'll talk to him."

"Oh no," Tom insisted, "you really don't have to do that for me."

"But I *want* to do that for you," Bobby said. "I mean, I understand the nature of all this and I can't say I entirely agree with any of it but there's a point at which it crosses the line, and I think Prest-O there just crossed the line."

"Well," Tom started, a bit lost for words, "know that I really, really appreciate that."

"No worries," Bobby said, before grinning a bit, "but you just may owe me a foot massage in return."

Tom also grinned. "Yeah, I think that's kind of a given."

The two boys continued typing away, Tom pretty much ignoring the fact that he hadn't had dinner yet (and, really, not wanting to leave his room lest he run into Preston again), and after about 15 minutes, Bobby turned to Tom, and, out of nowhere, simply asked:

"But Preston's feet were nice though, right?"

Tom appeared caught off guard by the sheer abruptness of the query, but responded with a deep, serious tone of voice: "Oh, like you wouldn't believe."

"So," Bobby continued, "who has the nicest feet here, then?"

"Um," Tom thought honestly, "I mean, it's hard to say. I kind of like the rugged aggressiveness of Matt's. They're 'straight' feet, ya know? Well-worn, properly smelly, but not overly rank or jock-y. I think I like his the most. Dave's I might like the least, just 'cos he never breaks 'em out: he rarely wears sandals, he's got really soft soles, which, I mean, is nice and everything, but you kind of want a bit more texture, to it, ya know? And Red's are ... well, I haven't spent as much time with his, but they're also pretty jock-y and tasty. Although I guess I'm going to be seeing him in about 45 minutes so I'm sure I'll have more full-formed opinion on them at that point."

A pause filled the room. Bobby was just staring at the guy in his room that had a slightly-smudged "PRESTON'S FOOTPIG" written across his forehead. A bit uneased, Tom queried back: "Um, why do you ask? I mean, Dave kind of already did that during the video filming session that one night."

"It's just so interesting to me," Bobby started, "'cos you describe feet like most snobs would describe wine, in textures and flavors and nuances. I just -- I dunno, I never really thought of feet as sexual in any way until I met you. So ... kudos? I guess?"

"I'll take that as a compliment," Tom smiled back.

"Should I even ask what Matt made you do?" Bobby said, turning back to his computer as he listened.

"I mean," Tom fumbled a bit, unsure if what he was going to say was publicly known, "I dunno. Have you ever heard of The Rooster?"

Bobby turned back to face Tom, mouth agape. "Oh my god, did you fucking meet The Rooster?"

"Yes!" Tom said excitedly. Bobby pulled his chair closer.

"We just keep hearing about it," Bobby started, "as some girls actually got high and 'met' him, as it were, but no one can ever get any details about it. It's, like, his biggest fantasy thing ever, so the fact that he wound up using it on you -- oh man, you have to tell me everything."

Tom sported a grin: "Can I rub your feet while I do so?"

"Hell yeah!" Bobby shouted back. Both boys immediately went to Bobby's bed to start this exchange.

A half-hour later, Bobby's jaw was still agape, stunned by the level of ridiculous detail Tom was able to provide in telling the tale of Matt becoming The Rooster, all while Tom's mouth gleefully spit out nuance after nuance, doing his best to (as always) hide his throbbing, raging footboner in his jeans as he felt up Bobby's beautiful, tender bare feet. Bobby had pretty much checked out of the notion of feet being weird, and Tom was very content with the understanding they had reached.

Tom skillfully left out the portion after the whole Rooster incident where he wound up stumbling back into Bobby's room and being caught jerking off to his socks, and it was that moment when he noticed the time. 5:47pm. Almost time to meet with Red.

"Sorry man," Tom started, releasing Bobby's sweet toes from his grip, "but I'm going to suffer under Red's rule now."

"You don't have to do this, ya know," Bobby offered. "I mean, I can talk to the guys. There's a way to get out of this."

"That's what my roommate's been telling me," Tom noted, thinking about he hadn't heard from Theron for a bit, which, sad as that was, was probably for the best.

"Well why don't you?" Bobby asked, getting out of his bed and plopping down in his computer chair.

"I don't know," Tom said, "I mean, Red's got everything already uploaded on the cloud and all sorts of things--"

"Which I am the administrator of," Bobby noted. "I mean, if that's all he's got out of you, taking that down will not be a hardship. Red trusts me 'cos I've been impartial this whole time, but christ man, you're a sex slave, basically. Like, that's not cool on ... so many levels."

"But what about Preston?" Tom inquired.

"Trust me," Bobby started, "Preston is not a worry. He thinks he's got stuff on you? I've got stuff on him. In fact, we *all* got stuff on him, and it is all ... quite, let's say, delicious. I don't know: delicious may not be the word. Just know there's enough to force his hand, if that's what you're concerned about."

Tom's mind was in a weird place: this was a genuine out. He could escape all of this. However, for whatever reason, he just felt ... hesitant about taking that step. In many ways, being in this environment has been absolute and total hell for him, being forced to do so many things that he didn't want to do. On the exact opposite end of that spectrum, he was getting more foot exposure than he had ever had in his life, and the things he was discovering, the hesitant walls of timidness that was preventing his sexuality from being truly explored were all coming down, opening up a new, better, more readily-embraced version of himself. Tom was ecstatic about all the new things he was trying, even as he was conscious of the cost of which it was all happening. Bobby's prospect was seriously enticing, but in the end, Tom felt he at least had to go through Red before he could make any sort of potential jailbreak.

"I'm sorry, Bobby," Tom started, "but I have to at least see through what Red wants to do to me. I know it sounds weird, but after that, let's seriously talk, OK? I mean, it sounds great, but ... I have to see this through. Final boss at the end of the level, ya know?"

There was another pause, but Bobby nodded his head. "I'm OK with this so long as you're serious about getting out of this once and for all."

"I am," Tom confirmed, actually meaning it.

"OK," Bobby said, his voice trailing off a bit, "but I gotta warn you: Red is nothing to mess with. I mean, he seems like the well-reasoned leader through all of this, but trust me, he can be devious beyond all words. Ask any of his exes: it's not about sex with him -- it's about power, and once he has power to wield over someone, the last thing he wants to do is to make anyone forget it. I don't know what he's got planned, but promise to see me right after, OK?"

"OK," Tom said. As if on cue, Tom's phone pinged with a text alert. He flipped it open: it was 6pm on the dot, and there was a message from Red saying "My room. Now."

"That him?" Bobby asked.

"None other," Tom said, taking a deep breath and walking towards the door.

"Good luck," Bobby said before turning to face his computer, "You're probably going to need it."

Right as he was out the door, Tom stopped for a second and turned back to Bobby. "You know," he started, "I won't lie that I came into this whole thing kind of having a crush on you, but man ... you're beyond that. Like, you're a genuinely good guy, and ... well, I appreciate that. Like, really."

Bobby stared at Tom, each genuine word hitting Bobby's ears with nothing but good intent. Bobby broke out a very small smile, but nodded his head. That's all Tom needed to see.

Tom walked out into the living room, a few guys hanging out and pulling up stuff on their tablets. As Tom turned to go up the staircase, a flip-flopped Preston was coming down. Preston was gazing at Tom's forehead, before noting "Very good, boy. A bit sweaty there, but very good."

"The Wheaties are on top of the fridge," Tom said as he passed Preston on the staircase.

"Even better news," Preston exalted, "You're gonna go far, kid!"

Tom smirked a bit, and finally reached the landing to the second floor. He found Red's door (the one with the words "The King" written on it on what he hoped was removable paint), took a deep breath, and knocked.

Ready or not, here we go.

CHAPTER TEN: RED-emption

"Come in!" Red shouted.

Tom opened up the door to see Red's room: it was remarkably clean and surprisingly large. There were two upright beds on either side of it (why one would need two beds is something Tom couldn't possibly fathom as to why) and directly from the entrance was a large three-paneled window alcove that gave a great view of the entire campus. In front of it was a computer with a two-monitor setup, the hardwood floor covered with a nice but indistinct rug. There were closets near the entrance but nary a loose piece of clothing anywhere to be found. Tom did notice a pair of slip-on soccer slides near the door, but those were nothing ... to what Red was wearing.

It wasn't too distinct a look: faded red T-shirt of a sports team Tom had never heard of (but, to be fair, he hasn't heard of a lot of sports teams), black boxing shorts that looked comfortable as all get-out, and some thick, meaty leather sandals containing Red's thick, meaty feet. Tom's eyes were drawn to those sandaled toes first and foremost, and then were drawn to what was in the center of the floor: a whole bunch of thick white ropes, perhaps the kind used for repelling down mountains and the like. Tom wasn't quite sure what to think but--

"Oh, so Preston got to ya, huh?" Red noted.

"Yeah, I ate his Wheaties not realizing they were his," Tom admitted.

"Yeah, that's a cardinal sin," Red joked, "but it sounds like he made you pay."

"Well yes ... that he did," said Tom, meekly.

"Well quite frankly, this is good for me," Red said with a lilt in his voice, "'cos it will only add to the stuff I have planned for you."

"What did you have in m--"

"Strip," Red ordered.

"But, I mean, like -- all the way?" asked Tom, a bit worried.

"I'm sorry, did I fucking stutter?" Red was menacing right now. "Strip!"

Tom didn't want to provoke the titan any more than was necessary. Slowly, he took off his clothes until he was completely naked save for the words "PRESTON'S FOOTPIG" smudged on his forehead. Suddenly, the fact that Red had a room with so many big windows facing the campus was starting to worry him (sure, they were only on the second floor, but still).

"Yeah, that's it, be the good naked little footpig I know you are," Red taunted.

"Yes ... sir," said Tom, unsure of exactly how to respond to that.

"Now," Red teased out, "lay face down on the floor and grab your ankles behind you."

"Yes sir," Tom said, again very unsure of what's going to happen. He laid his bare stomach on Red's carper and reached behind his back to grab his ankles. Red walked up to his face and slid off his sandals, then using his meaty toes to push them so both flops were directly in front of Tom's face. Tom could see that these things had been used extensively, the outline of Tom's footprints practically having been burned into these things, years of footsweat preserving his shape, form, and smell perfectly.

"Now here's how this is going to work," Red started, "I'm going to tie you up here, and you're going to lick the insides of my smelly sandals until I tell you to stop, OK?"

"Yes sir," Tom said, a bit excited by the prospect.

"Now!" Red ordered.

Tom needed no further encouragement: he got out his tongue and drug his first lap from the imprint of the ankle all the way up to the ball of the foot. Sweet *fuck* that was tasty! It was like all those smells of male feet in socks and by their sweaty selves had been compounded into this one set of sandals, and dear fuck if it didn't excite his mouth with flavor and his dick with pleasure. Suddenly, against the fear that Tom had upon entering the room and the feeling of Red's hands tying up his arms and legs in a tight hog-tied position, Tom was getting turned on and lost in the taste of Red's sandals. It was like each lick was telling him a bit more about the history of Red's feet: where they've been and where they were going. It was the most addictive thing ever: every lick only made Tom want to lick even more, and he was soon lapping at it like a dog with some peanut butter. Tom literally couldn't stop: he was loving the living fuck out of Red's footsweat on these well-worn leather sandals, and just wanted more and more and more.

"Here we go, boy!" Red shouted.

Suddenly, Tom was airborne. Tom was panicked for a moment, trying to figure out what was going on (and his tongue was mad at him for not licking those sandals anymore), but soon realized that not only did Red hog-tie him extremely tightly, but he must've had some sort of pulley system installed in the ceiling of his room, and was now lifting up the horny, naked, tightly bound Tom until he was about three, maybe four feet off the ground. Seemingly satisfied, Red tied the rope off so that Tom was simply hanging there, horny and hard, exposed in the open air of the room.

"Perfect," Red noted. He walked over to one of his closets and pulled out a pair of cheap flip-flops not too dissimilar to what Preston was wearing, and held one of them right up to Tom's nose.

"You like that?" Red asked.

Tom sniffed and his dick, again, twitched all on its own. "Yessur," Tom muffled out while in a state of ecstasy.

"Good," Red said, removing it and then hanging the sandal to Tom's erect cock by the toestrap, "then make sure this doesn't fall off, OK? I'm gonna go get set up."

Red went over to his computer as Tom's dick felt the light weight of that cheap flop hanging from his member, almost completely forgetting that the words "PRESTON'S FOOTPIG" were still smeared on his forehead. For whatever reason, having a physical totem like this -- in this case, Red's cheap sandal -- attached to his own raging footboner was hot in its own way. There wasn't a constant stimuli to help it like licking a sandal or smelling a sock, but in truth, just feeling the *weight* of that sandal on his cock was enough to keep it upright for the time being.

"Hello, campus!" Red suddenly declared. Tom looked over and saw Red was facing his computer screens, but couldn't make out exactly what was going on. It appeared Red was talking, maybe Skyping with somebody? Maybe a lot of people? Oh shit.

"I am Red and as some of you may or may not know, we have had a special guest here at the ol' TKL this past while, and I am excited to introduce all of you to him right now." Red stood up and gestured over to the suspended, hard, naked Tom. "I present to you ... Footpig!"

Tom was speechless. Now that Red had moved, Tom could see that, in fact, he was on some sort of webcam feed right now, and there he was, dangling with a flip-flop hanging from his shaft, "PRESTON'S FOOTPIG" still on his forehead (although Tom's nervous sweat was smudging it even more). This was not good.

"Yes," Red continued, in full showman mode, "this is a true-as-they-come Footpig, one who is helplessly addicted to the sights, sounds, and smells of male feet. You'll note that one of my own flip-flops is hanging from his junk right now." Red took a moment to tug at it a bit, although Tom's hardon snapped right back up when Red let go. "Oh yes, nice and horny. He was licking the insides of one of my other set of sandals earlier. You really loved that didn't you, Footpig?"

Tom was a bit aghast, flabbergasted. He could barely think of anything to say, much less regard who he was going to be saying anything to.

"Aww, don't be shy now, Footpig. You don't want me to read one of your letters out loud to the whole campus now do you?" Red teased.

"Yes, I really loved it!" Tom reflexively shouted.

"Ah yes," Red said, addressing what appeared to be the whole campus again. "Did you catch that bit of fear right there? This little Footpig first came to our attention when we stole his laptop and discovered just documents upon documents of his own little foot fetish confessions: all of the guys on campus whose exposed toes just make him nut all over the place. It's ... really embarrassing, isn't it, Footpig?"

"Yes it is," Tom said, still processing what was going on.

"And man, let me tell you guys, there are a lot of you on campus who would be surprised by just how badly this boy is crushing on yer toes. As you can see from his forehead, one of our own Brothers here managed to utilize him quite dutifully. You sure do love feet, don't ya, Footpig?"

"Yes," Tom gulped, "I do."

"That's what I'm talkin' about," Red smirked. "Now, he also has admitted that he is a ticklish little fuck, so, here's the idea I had, campus: let's interrogate him publicly here, and I'll tickle his wimpy naked body until he tells the truth. Sound good?"

Tom shook his head back and forth violently, indicating the sheer degree of not-cool this was, but being in the predicament he was, he didn't really have a choice. Red walked over to him and stood so he was almost eye-level with the hog-tied, suspended boy. He reached out and began lightly circling the tips of Tom's nipples with his index finger, causing his cock to twitch once again.

"Now tell me, Footpig," he started, "do you like my bare feet?"

Tom gave a guttural groan of pleasure against his will: "Yes sir, I do!"

"Very good!" said Red, still teasing those niptips. "What's your favorite part about them?"

Tom was again grimacing to try and mask the pleasure that Red was forcing into his body: "The smell! The taste! I fucking love the taste!"

"Oh yeah," Red said towards the camera, momentarily pausing his torment, "I should note that before I bound and suspended the Footpig here, he *really* enjoyed licking the insides of my sandals. Like, pathetically so. Oh man, you guys just have no idea. It was ... hilarious. Ain't that right, Footpig?"

"Yes sir," Tom said again.

"Now," Red started, turning his fingers again towards teasing Tom's nips, "why don't you name me all of the guys whose feet you wound up sucking on and licking just this week. How does that sound?"

Tom grimaced, trying to keep his mouth shut even as the torment continued.

"I said, how does that sound, Footpig?" Red now began lightly tapping his fingers on Tom's ribcage, and instantly Tom's body began shaking and vibrating, unable to control the tickles that were coming into it. "All I want are some namesy-wamesies, Footpig. We can make this easy. Have you licked *my* feet?"

A chortled laugh snuck out of Tom's mouth as he agreed: "Yessssss."

"Good," Red encouraged, still tickling his victim. "Now name another one."

"Matt!" Tom shouted, trying not to give in.

"Good," Red continued. "And another one?"

"Bobby!" Tom shouted.

Red stopped tickling him for a bit. "Wait a moment, you actually licked the feet of Bobby? The one who's been most opposed to this idea the whole time?"

Tom was already panting, that tickle attack having already taken a good deal out of him. "Yes."

"Well who else?" Red ordered, crossing his arms as he faced the bound boy.

"Dave, obviously. J.C. Theron."

"Oh that's right -- I remember that from our little filming session the other night," Red smirked. "For the record, I can't wait to see that finished product. It is going to be hotter than ballsacs, let me tell ya."

Tom arched his eyebrow a bit at the strange colloquialism, but was happy to be off topic even for a half-second.

"Who else?" Red demanded.

"Preston!" Tom shouted. Red moved in and started teasing his nipples.

"Oh I know that," Red started, his voice dropping to a guttural, sexy tone, "but I want to know ... who else?"

"I'd ... I'd rather not say," Tom said.

"Wrong answer," Red said. With that, he began digging his fingers hard into Tom's ribcage, and immediately, the boy started yelping. Laughter shot out of him like big cumshot, echoing across the room and immediately testing the limiter on the webcam's mic. It was wild, untamed laughter, arguably animalistic, and completely unhinged. Tom was able to get in the occasional shouts of "No!" or "Stop!" but those were often drowned out by the hyena sounds he was making all around them. It was downright manic, and undoubtedly scary to some of the campus denizens who were watching this right now.

"C'mon, Footpig!" Red demanded, "I'm not joking around here! You're holding out on a name! I want to know what it is! You better tell me or I'm going to email all of your laptop content to every email in the campus directory at the press of a button! You'll be a public Footpig for *life*! Do you want that? Do you want to be known as a Footpig on your permanent record?"

"No!" Tom shouted as Red's fingers tapped in the soft parts in-between each rib-bone to get the most laughter it could out of his Footpig pinata.

"Then tell me!" Red shouted. "Tell me the name or you're finished!"

Tom knew the name: it was Christopher. It was the drug dealer he scored weed off of and the last possible person he would want to expose, as not only was he a nice guy, but if Red asked him the context as to why he worshiped his feet, it could bring even worse consequences for him. Even at his horniest, Tom tried to be a man of morals, and this one name was one he didn't want to give up, although the endless, inescapable cascade of tickles that were being levied upon him were almost too much for him to handle. He could feel his own conscious cracking a bit. This was overwhelming. Tom literally couldn't take it anymore.

"Ch--" Tom choked out.

"Yes! Tell me the whole name!" Reds shouted with a maniacal glee in his eyes.

"Ch--" Tom reluctantly tried again.

"Just fucking tell me already!" Red screamed.

At that moment, Red's door flung open. It was Theron.

"Stop whatever the fuck you're doing!" Theron shouted.

"The fuck are you?" Red shot back, stopping his tickling of Tom to acknowledge this intruder.

"I'm Tom's roommate and I'm getting him out of here." Theron immediately went over to where the pulley system was and began untying the rope.

"Ha!" Red smirked, "You're the one who, lemme guess, had your toes in Footpig's mouth here." Red faced his webcam. "Well, campus friends, it's unfortunate that Footpig has friends, 'cos right now, I'm about to launch out all sorts of stuff we have stored up on our internal cloud server. Sorry, Footpig, but your life is over."

"No!" Tom shouted, while panting. As he did so, his body began to slowly descend, as Theron was able to undue the rope and was lowering him down via the pulleys right through to a gentle landing on the carpet of Red's room. Red was fidgeting with something on the computer while Theron began untying his hogtied roommate.

"You're putting your clothes on and we're leaving, OK?" Theron said, untying the knots. Tom bent and flexed his appendages as each one was allowed motion again. After being bound so tight for such a long period of time, being able to stretch those muscles again was a welcome sensation.

"Oh sure," Red noted, clicking on more than a few things, "have fun leaving. Just know you're entering into a world where Footpig's reputation has just been emailed to every single email on the campus server. Students, professors, campus security, even the janitorial staff. I'm sorry boy, but you didn't play by the rules, and you will never, ever, ever live this thing down."

Tom was standing and almost through muscle memory began putting his boxers, pants, and shirt back on. Theron supervised and then shot a look back to Red: "You sure about that?"

Red arched his eyebrow a bit. The fuck did Tom's roommate know about this? Theron grabbed Tom by the shoulder and escorted him out of the room, down the staircase, and out the door of the frat. As they crossed the street back to the building that house Tom & Theron's room, Tom could actually hear a very loud, very audible scream come back from the frat house. It was definitely in Red's voice, too, although he had no idea what that was all about.

+ + +

As the two young men made their way back to their room, Theron placed the key in the door and opened it up.

"Welcome back home, buddy," Theron said.

As Tom entered the room, he saw that someone else was already in there: it was Bobby.

"Hey there, champ," Bobby said, greeting Tom warmly and openly. Tom looked around: Bobby's computer and most of his things were back to where they once were. Tom looked over to the desk that he had previously cleared out when he left and his phone, charger, laptop, and duffel bag were all there. Tom was befuddled.

"What ... what is going on here, guys?" Tom asked, surveying everything.

"I think you could use a beer, Tom," Theron declared. "You, Bobby?"

"Normally I don't drink," Bobby said, clad in jeans and trashy old black sneakers this time out, "But I think I could make an exception."

Theron grabbed a few and directed Tom to sit in a new beenbag that he must have gotten in the inexplicable disappearance of his roommate over the past few days. Theron grabbed his usual chair which faced the TV, Bobby sat in the chair that accompanied Tom's desk, and Tom laid back in the beanbag chair. Drinks were distributed all around.

"So," Tom asked after taking his first cautious swig, "what happened, guys?"

"Well," Theron started, taking charge of the conversation, "I got a chat from our good friend Bobby here, who decided to fill me in on what you were getting into tonight. In fact, he filled me in on ... all of your activities that you had since you started your, ahem, engagement at the Frat."

"Like," Tom asked carefully, "*all* of them?"

"Well," Bobby interjected, "all the ones that he needed to concern himself with."

"Ah," Tom noted, nervously taking another swig from the beer.

"Use this," Bobby said, tossing Tom a rag to wipe his forehead with.

"Thanks," Tom said, his own sweat making his forehead moist enough to get Preston's declarative message off his face pretty quickly.

"And, well," Theron continued, "when I heard that you were going to be Red's ... um ... property for the night? Well I knew that couldn't be good."

"And, knowing what I know about Red," Bobby added, "I knew he was going to use the stuff he had swiped from your hard drive and uploaded onto the cloud. Being concerned for your well-being, I figured Theron & I could be of assistance."

"So," Theron continued, "I knew to come by some time after ... whatever Red started doing what he was doing. Kind of lucked out a bit, I'd say, wouldn't you?"

"Yeah," laughed Bobby. All three men took another swig from their beers.

"So while I did that," Tom started, "Bobby graciously began moving his stuff over to my place, because he knew full well that what Red was planning was stuff that, once stopped, no one wanted to be around to feel the wrath of. He did that and I helped a bit, and then I made my grand entrance."

"But guys," Tom said with a panicked tone in his voice, "you don't understand: he was broadcasting this out to the entire campus. It's like he had his own web show or something. Then he ... ugh, I think he emailed out all the ... all the stuff I wrote. Like, all of it."

Theron & Bobby gave each other knowing glances.

"I can confirm that he did send out a link to the contents of all the stuff stored on the shared frat cloud server to the entire campus," Bobby noted, smiling, "but I highly doubt he double-checked the actual files themselves before he did so."

Tom's eyes widened. He couldn't believe what he was hearing.

"So," Tom started piecing it together, "you swapped out the files that were on my hard drive?"

"Maybe," Bobby teased.

"Are there any records of my files anymore?"

"Nope," chuckled Bobby.

"Well ... what did you put in its place?" asked Tom, eager for answers.

"Well, remember when I said that I had stuff on Preston? Well, I not only, ahem, 'convinced' Preston to delete that video, but I also managed to hack the computers of Matt, Dave, and Red, and found some ... rather humiliating photos and videos of all of them. I mean, say what you will about those guys, but they are narcissists, and they do enjoy evidence of themselves in the act, as it were."

A pause filled the room.

"So when Red emailed every address on the campus server, he emailed everyone ... stuff that he and Matt and Dave all thought was private?" Tom asked.

"Maybe," teased Bobby once more.

"But ... I mean ... what about the webcam?"

"Funny thing about web broadcasts," Bobby said as he guzzled more beer, "they don't really work all that well when your computer is being fed a fake signal indicating that you're broadcasting."

"So ... no one saw a second of it?" Tom asked, a smile growing across his face.

"Not even me," said Bobby.

Tom was just ... overwhelmed with emotion right now. He couldn't believe it. His roommate and ... well, his new friend -- they just went to bat for him and freed him from the most heinous, evil thing he had ever been dragged into. He couldn't recall any time anyone had ever "stood up" for him, and he was almost to tears.

"Thank you guys," Tom said, getting up and going to hug each one of them separately. "I ... don't even know how to repay you."

"You'll think of something," Bobby noted.

"A foot rub?" Tom asked.

"Ha," Bobby snorted, "I mean, Tom ... there are other ways to thank someone aside from offering them a foot massage, ya know?"

A pause hit the air. Tom wasn't quite sure what Bobby meant, so his impulses took over, and he briefly leaned in to give Bobby a kiss. It was quick, and as he pulled back, Tom could see Bobby's face was very surprised.

"Um, that's not what I had in mind either," Bobby said, "but, um ... thanks? I guess?"

"You can buy the next round of beers," Theron suggested.

"Yeah," Tom said, a bit embarrassed by this kiss to Bobby. "I can do that."

"Oh fuck it," Bobby said, "I *could* use a foot massage, but do that while we're watching a movie or something."

"Fair enough," Theron said, pulling out his DVD binder to find something fitting. Tom meanwhile repositioned his beanbag so it was right in front of the chair Bobby was in. Bobby put his sneakered feet down, resting right on Tom's chest, and Tom began unlacing the shoes to get ready. Theron made a few quizzical faces at his roommate's actions, but figured it was better Tom be here than over at the Frat house.

The boys didn't end up going to sleep until well past midnight, swapping stories and tales and drinking all the while. Tom didn't even remember falling asleep.

+ + +

The next morning, Tom woke up in his own bed, a little bit hungover but not for any real need to be concerned. Theron was already gone, and Tom noticed Bobby in flip-flops and a towel wrapped around him, exiting the room to go take a shower. Tom raced through all the memories of what had happened through this past week and couldn't believe any of them were real. He had been degraded, humiliated, tormented and exposed, but in doing so, not only learned a lot more about his own needs and wants, but also really wound up learning who his real friends are.

He plugged in his laptop and fired it up, immediately checking his campus email. Amidst all the general "campus news" stuff, teacher emails, and updates on what was being served in the cafeteria at lunch today, Tom noticed a small and short email from the campus offices about an incident involving the members of the TKL fraternity. The message simply read that three members of that fraternity, "Red", Dave, and Matt, had all been suspended pending further investigation. Tom moved through his emails and found that there was an earlier one from ... what appeared to be Red's address. "Check this out!" it read in the headline along with a link to a link on his cloud server. Tom kind of wanted to open it up just to see what Bobby had gathered ... but thought better of it. Being mean and prying on other people's personal lives was those guys' M.O., not Tom's. He kind of wanted to check and see if Bobby really did what he said he did, but trusted him. After all he went through last night, he felt a lot better.

The door opened and a dried-off and toweled Bobby wound up coming back in to put his shower bucket full of shampoos and the like away. Despite the audible sound of those sandals slapping at his heels, Tom didn't turn to look, instead keeping up on his emails and trying to figure out a plan of attack for the day. As he typed and clicked, he didn't notice Bobby come up behind him and lean in to ear.

"So," Bobby started, "about that kiss last night ..."

Tom's smile grew wider than it ever had before.

THE END

HOW TO BE A FOOTPIG

1. Acknowledge you are a footpig.

It may seem surprisingly simple, but there are those who go about
their life with a deep-seated male foot fetish that they, for whatever
reason, keep locked up inside. It's an urge they fight, something they
to suppress, etc. I tried fighting it for years, but it was a losing battle.
The second I accepted this part of me, the second I embraced it
wholeheartedly and just fucking *loved* this aspect of myself, my life
got so much better to an almost incalculable degree. It felt like a
weight had been lifted, and now I just fucking *love* male feet with
all my heart. Accept it in your own heart, and life is gonna get a
whole lot easier for you.

2. Don't overdo it.

Strange as it may be, there is a thing called being "too much" of a
footpig. It's the thing where you just interject it into everyday
conversations when no one asked you to. No one wants to be known
around the office as "the foot guy" -- so mark your spots carefully.
Tell only those whom you feel are truly trustworthy with this
information. Despite your perverse, too-powerful fetish, don't forget
that you're also a regular person with interests or and attributes all
your own that make you unique. As a side-note, it's also good to
know not to be taken advantage of either: if a footdom presents you
with something like financial domination and that just ain't your bag,
then <u>don't go through with it</u>. The need to serve feet is
unquestionably powerful, but never lose yourself in the middle of it.
If that's your thing, then go with it all-in. If you feel you're being
dragged to places that are genuinely (not playfully) uncomfortable,
then pull out. You may be a footpig, but even footpigs have *some*
dignity.

3. Drink it all in.

Whether you're at an office with a loose dress code or you're in the
middle of the streets when it's summer, realize that male feet are all
around you all the time. Look but don't leer. Drink it in but don't

give yourself up. Absorb all these tastes, shapes, and flavors, as you'll soon realize that the best thing about being a footpig is that it is a frequent, constant, unstoppable thing, and in many ways that's wonderful. You don't have to be a freak about it, but just acknowledge that feet are all around you and are there for you to absorb into your footpig brain.

4. Are you a sub or a dom?

It may seem like a simple question, but there are some guys with foot fetishes that eventually take great joy in being able to manipulate the wills and spirits of those around them with nothing more than a flick of their toes. The feeling of being worshiped is great, and even if you are a sub, reach out to those even more pathetic than you to slurp your own toes because it's important to know what that feeling is like, along with what works and what doesn't technique-wise. If you're serving someone's feet, it's important to make sure they are constantly stimulated: the same back-and-forth toe-suck action will eventually make the master's mind get bored, a repetition without variation is a very boring thing indeed.

5. Build up confidence in other's feet.

As you go about your life as a footpig, acknowledging the power of all the male feet around (and rest assured, they are powerful), you'll like meet the friend who, for whatever reason, just hates their feet, or perhaps just hates feet in general. They think feet are boxy, disgusting, unwieldy -- you name it. Of course, you know full well that this is complete and total bullshit, 'cos you are a footpig and you've *seen* OK or average or even "bad" feet before, and you know full well what good feet look like. If your friend has a good pair but seems to be dismissive of it, don't be afraid to push a compliment their way. Obviously, saying "nice feet" can sound a bit weird out of context, but you can say things like "Dude, trust me, your feet are not that bad," in response to some off-handed comment they make. Even a slight interjection like that followed by a quick topic change may just very well plant that seed in their brain that allows it to grow, leading them to out-and-out foot confidence. Don't labor on it too much, but prop up the feet of others until (and this happened to me before), they finally do say "Yeah, my feet *are* sexy, aren't they?" Damn right they are. Get them to that point and make them realize that their feet can be powerful, appreciated things (got that, Adam?).

6. Acknowledge the most powerful of truths.

In a physiological sense, the parts of the brain that recognize genitalia and feet are incredibly close together, and very frequently there is a cross of wires that happens, which leads not only to people like you having a foot fetish, but also explains why over one third of body fetishes worldwide in any gender/orientation revolve around feet in some way. If you have a foot fetish, there is a very, very good chance you're going to have it for the rest of your life -- so do yourself a favor and just get used to it. Per Rule #1, embracing it is key, so don't be scared by the fact you'll have this forever: accept it and love it. It's a great thing to have. After all, in case you didn't know already ...

7. Suck for *his* pleasure -- not your own.

It's incredibly easy to simply have a pair of masculine toes that you merely suck on for hours on end -- but that accounts for almost nothing if you're unable to please the person they're attached to as well. Mix up your style, try some new things, and really highlight the sheer erogenous nature of bare feet to the best that you can, focusing on *his* pleasure points and *his* hot spots as well. The right amount of mouth manipulation can actually lead to how own moaning and throbbing, and that's exactly the way to do it.

8. Feet = happiness.

Even with you being a footpig, you will still go on to meet good people, have great relationships, and overall just have good times with your life well outside the fetish. However, there will *also* be those times where you reach euphoric, horny highs where you realize that feet are just perfect. They're great to look at, amazing to taste, and deserve all the appreciation and cumshots you can give them. Feet are a powerful, sexy force and can make you happy even in your darkest hour. It's the comfort of having a go-to fetish. It will be there for you as you feed it. Don't be afraid of it: embrace it! And rest assured, this fetish will treat you well in return.

OTHER WORKS BY JAMES T. MEDAK

+ + +

How To Be a Tickle Slave (2010)

My, What Ticklish Feet You Have (2012)

Getting Off on the Wrong Foot (2013)

The Best Foot Forward: The James T. Medak Anthology (2014)

40776617R00105

Made in the USA
San Bernardino, CA
28 October 2016